Prodigal Moon

Prodigal Moon

Walt Cross

Dire Wolf Books

Stillwater, Oklahoma

Dire Wolf Books
An Imprint of Cross Publications
502 E. Liberty Avenue
Stillwater, OK 74075

First Paperback Edition 2016

ISBN: 978-0-9850996-5-7

For Justin and Alex both of whom are science fiction aficionados. And for Carol, who listens patiently to my stories. Additionally, it is written in memory of my brother Don Cross, a sailor aboard the real *USS Trathen*, and who left us too soon.

Walt Cross

Calendar Used in *Prodigal Moon*

2049 with Significant Dates Indicated

January
Su	Mo	Tu	We	Th	Fr	Sa
					1	2
3	4	5	6	7	8	9
10	11	12	13	14	15	16
17	18	19	20	21	22	23
24	25	26	27	28	29	30
31						

February
Su	Mo	Tu	We	Th	Fr	Sa
	1	2	3	4	5	6
7	8	9	10	11	12	13
14	15	16	17	18	19	20
21	22	23	24	25	26	27
28						

March
Su	Mo	Tu	We	Th	Fr	Sa
	1	2	3	4	5	6
7	8	9	10	11	12	13
14	15	16	17	18	19	20
21	22	23	24	25	26	27
28	29	30	31			

April
Su	Mo	Tu	We	Th	Fr	Sa
				1	2	3
4	5	6	7	8	9	10
11	12	13	14	15	16	17
18	19	(20)	21	22	23	24
25	26	27	28	29	30	

Discovery of Barcia's Planet

May
Su	Mo	Tu	We	Th	Fr	Sa
						1
2	3	4	5	6	7	8
9	10	11	12	13	14	15
16	17	18	19	20	21	22
23	24	25	26	27	28	29
30	31					

June
Su	Mo	Tu	We	Th	Fr	Sa
		1	2	3	4	5
6	7	8	9	10	11	12
13	14	15	16	17	18	19
20	21	22	23	24	25	26
27	28	29	30			

July
Su	Mo	Tu	We	Th	Fr	Sa
				1	2	3
4	5	6	7	8	9	10
11	12	13	14	15	16	17
18	19	20	21	22	23	24
25	26	27	28	29	30	31

August
Su	Mo	Tu	We	Th	Fr	Sa
1	2	3	4	5	6	7
8	9	10	11	12	13	14
15	16	17	18	19	20	21
22	23	24	25	26	27	28
29	30	31				

September
Su	Mo	Tu	We	Th	Fr	Sa
			(1)	2	3	4
5	6	7	8	9	10	11
12	13	14	15	16	17	18
19	20	21	22	23	24	25
26	27	(28)	29	30		

1st Landing, Sovereignty Day

October
Su	Mo	Tu	We	Th	Fr	Sa
					1	2
3	4	5	6	7	8	9
10	11	12	13	14	15	16
17	18	19	20	21	22	23
24	25	26	27	28	29	30
31						

November
Su	Mo	Tu	We	Th	Fr	Sa
	1	2	3	4	5	6
7	8	9	10	11	12	13
14	15	16	17	18	19	20
21	22	23	24	25	26	27
28	29	30				

December
Su	Mo	Tu	We	Th	Fr	Sa
			1	2	3	4
5	6	7	8	9	10	11
12	13	14	15	16	17	18
19	20	21	22	23	24	25
26	27	28	29	30	31	

Main Characters

Dr. Trish Barcia, discoverer of Barcia's Planet
Dr. Halberd Boyle, planetary geology
William Tiberius Carswell, PODUS
LTC John Cummings, pilot
CPT Jacque D'Artan ESA pilot
Dr. Rolf Earhart, astronomy
Dr. Isadora Fontana, ESA biologist
Dr. Marjorie Fox, botany, agriculture
COL Chao Cheng Li, pilot Chinese mission
Dr. Daniel O'Brian, head of NASA mission
Dr. Hans (Hank) Russell, director of NASA
Dr. George Stanford, director of CIA
Dr. Nigel St. John, head of ESA mission
Commander Phillip Tucker, *USS Trathen*
Dr. Boris Volkov, director of Russspace
COL Borya Zolner, Russspace

Source: Encyclopedia of Space Exploration, page 456, Volume IX, opening introduction.

Barcia's Planet

The wandering planet named *Barcia's Planet* was first detected on April 20, 2049 by the Martian Observatory Team (MOT) at NASA's Barsoom Station located on the edge of the Chryse Planitia, or 'golden plain' of Mars. Situated almost exactly midway between the *Pathfinder* and *Viking 1* landing sites, the station was a small colony of scientists living in the station itself and a number of connected life support domes. The MOT at the time was under the direction of Dr. Daniel O'Brian and consisted of Dr. O'Brian and five other astronaut scientists.

Hal Boyle planetary science, Trish Barcia science officer, Colonel John Cummings pilot, Rolf Earhart astronomer, and Marjorie Fox exobotanist, all of whom worked with the *Copernicus* telescope in geosynchronous orbit high above the Red Planet.

At the time of detection *Copernicus* was trained on a planetary system many light years away. Dubbed *Copernicus 12*, the system consisted of a number of rocky planets orbiting a red dwarf star. Smaller and cooler than Earth's sun, the system's planets huddled close to their small star in tight orbits, as if consciously seeking its warmth. Of the seven planets orbiting the star two were in the so called 'Goldilocks Zone', that just right area not too hot or too cold for possible life to have developed. Both planets were near Earth-size. *Copernicus* was trained on the system for nearly two Martian months and a good deal of data was accumulating in the science station's computer systems for analysis and eventual transmission to Earth. This lag in time gave the team a chance to see most of what new information there was before it moved on to others. They were on the forefront of planetary research.

APRIL 20, 2049
MARS OBSERVATION TEAM
BARSOOM STATION, MARS

Trish Barcia had just begun her shift relieving Rolf Earhart at the console scanning visual data input gathered and transmitted to the station by the *Copernicus* space telescope. Rolf stretched his six foot frame, raising his arms above his head and exaggerating his yawn as he looked down at Trish. His northern European descent was evident in his dark blonde hair and blue eyes. "Too bad we can't grab a little breakfast together Trish." He said, "Our shifts are always opposite one another, it's as if you are avoiding me." He continued, chuckling.

Trish glanced at him, "Not at all Rolf, I'm not avoiding you. There are only so many of us and we have to… what the hell!" She said in a startled voice that brought Rolf instantly back to focus on the screen.

"What is it?" He asked, leaning over her shoulder to see the display. "I don't see anything other than what we've been seeing."

"There, on the left of the screen, it looks… it looks like an eighth planet wandering way outside the *Copernicus 12* sun system." She continued.

"Yes, it does." Rolf agreed. "But such a small star shouldn't have the gravity to hold a planet that far out, and it's such a tiny planet too!"

"It's not holding it Rolf, look at the Doppler; it's showing a blue shift. This object is not a part of *Copernicus 12*, it's a wanderer, and it is moving toward us!" She exclaimed.

Rolf's voice became a little hoarse as he swallowed and said "Better wake up Doctor Dan and I mean now!"

Daniel O'Brian had earned degrees at both MIT and Harvard but his colleagues often just called him Doc. Despite his many credentials including 10 years as an astronaut he had a free and smooth-going nature about him that made people feel at ease. As was a noted habit of his he reached up to his dark brown hair with its slightly graying fringe and scratched his head in wonder.

"That's quite an anomaly you two have come up with." He said. How long have you been watching it?"

"Actually Doc, it was Trish that first spotted it, I had left the console and was only a witness." Rolf replied.

Doc's dark and somewhat bushy eyebrows rose quizzically as he turned his gaze to Trish. "Is that so

Trish? Then I hereby designate it *Copernicus* 13, "Barcia's Planet".

New to the Mars station and self conscious of it, the pretty, pixie nosed, auburn haired scientist and trained astronaut in her own right, blushed. "Well, ah, I did see it but I haven't been here long and Rolf had just stepped away…"

Doc straightened up with a smile. "None of which matters a whit, Rolf will be remembered in the telling of this story as the guy who stepped away a moment too early. *Barcia's Planet* it is." Doc said, turning and smiling at his younger teammate.

Rolf smiled back a little crookedly and nodded.

"Why don't you go get the esteemed Dr. Hal Boyle and tell him I'd like him to step down here and do a little astrometrics, maybe find out where this wandering orb wandered in from?"

"Sure Doc, but I'd like to remain awhile despite my shift being over, this is pretty exciting." Rolf replied emphatically and stepped through the hatchway into the corridor.

Although it was getting near dawn, it might as well have been in the middle of the Martian night. What atmosphere Mars had provided very little diffusion of the sun's light, so there was little hint of the coming sunrise. Rolf glanced out at the barren rock and sand landscape lighted by Phobos, the bigger of Mars' two moons. From Rolf's vantage point on Mars Phobos appeared about one-third the size of Earth's moon but was in fact much smaller than that. Deimos, the smaller moon would appear soon but was so small it looked like a very bright star from the planet's surface.

Despite the fact he had now been on Mars for over a year, Rolf was still intrigued by the alien vista. Stopping before Hal's quarters, he tapped on the door, perhaps a little louder than he meant to, his excitement manifesting itself through the resulting load knocking.

Inside his one man room Hal had just finished viewing a private message from his personal console. He was still smiling from the chorus of "We miss you Grandpa and love you too!" from his two granddaughters, Alex and Anya, when the abrupt knocking made him jump. It was rare to hear a loud noise on Mars and when you did, it usually wasn't good news. He reached and opened the door exclaiming "What on Mars!"

There Rolf stood grinning from ear to ear. "That's almost exactly what Trish said Hal! Hope I didn't startle you, but Trish has made an important find, come on, Doc wants you on astrometrics and probably spectrum analysis too!" Rolf exclaimed.

In a nervous gesture Hal brushed back his nonexistent hair on his bald pate, pushed his sliver rimmed glasses back up his nose, and followed Rolf, too surprised to say a word. "More than a year at Barsoom Station and now something is really happening!" He thought.

"Trish, how long has it been since you first saw the image?" Doc asked.

Trish looked at the screen, "Six minutes, 23 seconds". She replied.

"So, it will be what, another twelve minutes at this distance before Earth gets the image of this thing transmitted by *Copernicus*?" Doc asked rhetorically. "And that's assuming someone is watching as close as you were. Okay, let's send a message of our own. Write this entry into the station log and forward a copy to NASA at Houston." Doc said, handing her a hand written note he'd scribbled as he talked.

Barsoom Station, Mars

Universal date April 20, 2049

At 07:10 hours Mars time this date visual contact was made with a planet sized object. Blue shift

Doppler readings indicate the object is moving on the outer fringe of the solar system in the general direction of Sol. This object is designated *Copernicus 13* – "Barcia's Planet" in honor of its discoverer Dr. Trish Elizabeth Barcia of this station. It is not, I repeat not, a part of *Copernicus 12*, astrometrics and spectrum analysis to follow.

O'Brian
Head of Station

With trembling fingers Trish typed in the message as written. She understood that from this moment on, her life would never be the same.

What she didn't realize was that no one's life would ever be the same, not on Mars, not on the Moon Colony, not on the research space stations around a number of Saturn's moons, not even on the Earth itself.

APRIL 20, 2049
BARSOOM STATION, MARS
BARCIA PLANET DISCOVERY PLUS 0 DAYS

Dr. Marjorie Fox, a lithe blonde haired woman with a keen intellect as well as a shapely figure, was just the kind of woman John Cummings was attracted to. As the land rover the two of them rode in slowly left the lights of Barsoom Station in the darkness behind, he racked his brain for a way to get closer to Marjorie.

A handsome ruggedly built man with a constant five o'clock shadow, John was exactly what the public expected an astronaut to look like. Although he had come in on the supply ship that brought Trish Barcia, in fact the ship he piloted, he'd struck out with her, a fact he blamed on the presence of three European Space Agency astronauts that hitched a ride to their own science station on Mars.

This pre-dawn geology trip was the first time he'd gotten alone with Marjorie since his arrival. And although protocol required them to remain inside their pressurized suits even inside the equally pressurized rover, he had hopes of convincing her to shed some of that outer wear.

The only member of Barsoom Station without the title of Dr. in front of his name, he had gotten his degree in aeronautical engineering at Texas A & M. He entered the Air Force out of ROTC directly after his graduation. Now a lieutenant colonel and trained astronaut his hopes were this mission to Mars would earn him the silver eagle of a full colonel. But right now the still single aero spaceman had another objective in mind. He turned to Marjorie, prepared to make his opening gambit, when the radio crackled with the sound of Rolf Earhart's voice.

"Hey you two, Doc would like you to return to station, big things are happening here. Is he being a good boy Marjorie?" He asked in a mischievous voice.

Marjorie glanced at John through her helmet's visor. "Why you askin' Rolf, you're not a little jealous are you?" She shot back. "Never mind, Colonel Cummings has been a complete gentleman. I don't know what big things you guys got going but okay, Rover 1 returning to Barsoom Station." She replied, not knowing how close her rejoinder to Rolf came to the truth, because indeed the handsome astronaut was somewhat jealous.

"No, not jealous, just checking… you guys come directly to the conference table in the messhall; Doc wants a meeting of the minds." Rolf continued in an abashed tone.

"I wonder what that's all about." John said, slowing the rover down and beginning a wide turn back toward the station, the bright headlights of the rover cut through the darkness and flashed across the rock-strewn terrain.

Marjorie pulled out her trip log and began to write in it. NASA was nothing if not a stickler for details. And Marjorie, as a scientist, was quite used to that.

Her background in geology, astronomy, and agriculture rounded off the corners of an Oklahoma cowgirl. Growing up in the small college town of Stillwater, She had originally intended to become a grade school teacher and so, got her degree in education at Oklahoma State. But after a year of teaching she found herself restless, needing a bit more action in her life. Brushing off a number of would-be suitors she went on to get her advanced degrees.

'Well, it sounds like something more exciting than a backed up hydroponics bay has got them going this morning." She said. Then she looked up as the sun, with little to no warning, climbed abruptly above the horizon, its harsh light causing her visor to suddenly darken protectively.

"Aw, jeez… that takes some getting used to." John said gesturing at the fiercely glowing orb.

"Yeah, despite the increased distance from the sun it shines fiercer here than on any Earth side desert." Marjorie said. "But it works well on the greenhouses; we grow a lot of veggies here. Good thing too, because the only protein we get besides our own grown peanuts is the freeze dried meat packets shipped in on each supply run. See if you can't get this thing to go a little faster, I'm curious what's causing all the hubbub."

The rest if the MOT team shuffled their notepads and clicked their pens impatiently while sitting around the dining table. They were waiting for Doc and Hal to arrive with the latest information on the wandering planet. The remains of a late breakfast were still on the table, open foil packets that once contained reconstituted bacon and eggs, recyclable dishes, cups, and eating utensils.

While the late comers ate, Trish and Rolf filled the two rover travelers in as soon as they arrived from securing the rover and shedding their pressurized suits. John and Marjorie read over the message sent to Earth as they sipped hot mugs of instant coffee.

"Good work Trish." Marjorie said, and was echoed by John. But to most of their many questions all she and Rolf could reply were "We don't know."

Finally they heard the distant conversation and footsteps of Doc and Hal coming down the station's main corridor. They swept into the room with Doc grinning and Hal with a rather comical face made up of a smile, muted with a frown, a look not easily achieved. They took seats at either end of the rectangular table, the usual positions unofficially reserved for both Doc, as the leader of MOT and Hal, the senior astronaut. Both lay a thin stack of documents on the table.

"Well, I'm glad you two weren't very far off when we called you back. Sorry we had to interrupt your excursion, but I thought you'd like to be here for this. I assume Trish and Rolf outlined what has happened and you've read our transmission to Earth. Of course our European colleagues at Darwin Station called us right away after viewing the data and congratulated us on Trish's discovery. And NASA as well as the president has responded in a message I am about to read to you."

President William T. Carswell has the honor to join with NASA in extending congratulations to the Martian Observatory Team and in particular to Dr. Trish Barcia upon her momentous discovery of *Copernicus 13,* "Barcia's Planet". It is a job well done!

NASA has reviewed the images transmitted by *Copernicus* and excitedly awaits any further developments as you are able to analyze *Barcia's Planet.*

Hans Albert Russell
Head of NASA

"So, having caught their attention, we need to put aside all considerations except those that impact our immediate well being, and concentrate on this new find. Dr. Boyle has some preliminary astrometrics and spectrum analysis he will share with us now. I temper your expectations a bit by adding it is yet early in the analysis, and it has a bit or a lot, of good news, bad news flavor to it, Hal."

As all eyes turned toward him as Hal shuffled his papers self consciously.

"I haven't had time yet to assemble the obligatory slide presentation, but I can give you some basic facts. The very curious and 'good' news is about the spectrum analysis. If all you Trekkies remember the often used planetary classification system on Star Trek, *Copernicus 13* is a class 'M' planet!" He exclaimed.

Someone was expected to say it, and it was Rolf. "What is Star Trek, and what is a class 'M' planet?" He asked innocently.

As a second generation American of German origin he had not been steeped in the legendary TV, film, and book history that is the science fiction series 'Star Trek'.

"What is Star Trek?" Someone chuckled, loud enough for all to hear.

Hal also chuckled. "Star Trek is not important right now Rolf, but a class 'M' is a planet that has the necessary raw materials to be a habitable world."

At the gasp that went around the table Hal held up his hand. "Don't get me wrong, *Barcia's Planet* still needs to climb some rungs to make it to the top of the ESI"

Hal got some vacant stares, although Marjorie nodded knowingly, and Hal clarified for the others. "The ESI or Earth Similarity Index is a classification system in planetary science. The missing ingredients for *Barcia's Planet* however, mainly involve its current distance from the warm cuddly zone next to a sun."

After more grins around the table Trish said. "What does that actually mean?"

Hal paused. "It means that the spectrum analysis indicates this wandering planet has very near the same levels of oxygen, nitrogen and, although it is an ice world at this time, an abundance of water that is nearly equal to those of Earth."

The buzz rose even greater than before as all the scientists except Hal and Doc were conversing. It was Doc that finally held up his hand and said "People, people, there is more. Please go on Dr. Boyle." He invited, the seriousness of the matter causing him to revert to Hal's more formal title.

"I stress again these are preliminary readings, the planet is still outside the orbit of Pluto, as it penetrates deeper into the solar system its atmosphere will become more gaseous as it heats up and we will know more." Again he paused.

"Now, as to the astrometrics… it is unlikely that *Barcia's Planet* is a wandering planet that just happened to get close enough to our system to enter it. It is in an orbit around the sun just like all the other planets. It only differs in the size of its orbit and the time it takes to complete that orbit.

Extrapolating with the little I know and stirred together with a lot of conjecture, I think *Barcia's Planet* completes an orbit, or one of its years, every 2.5 million of ours!"

This time the amazing revelation just brought silence, as if they had all been struck dumb, then Doc filled the silence.

"What that means guys, is the last time *Barcia's Planet* approached the sun, humans as we know them, did not yet walk the planet! The only eyes close to human that might have witnessed its last return were simian. Perhaps some forebears of great apes, and us, looked up, saw the passing planet and wondered 'What the hell! I say that because Hal's astrometrics indicates *Barcia's Planet* is on a course for a near approach rendezvous with Earth!"

For the second time the group was struck dumb. Just yesterday they were so busy with the vitally important but mundane running of a science station. Today, they were discovering and sending on to Earth, literally, earth shaking news. Their thoughts were a jumble.

"I know there is much more to talk about, and we'll get to it. But right now I want Hal to send his preliminary findings on to NASA, no doubt our European colleagues are coming to some of the same conclusions we are, and I want to get this to our folks first. But I will say one more thing. Hal holds out the possibility, and I agree with him, that *Barcia's Planet* has sped by planets of our solar system, Earth, and the sun at least 25 times in the past, and this will be the 26th!

I'll save you the math. All the evidence suggests that *Barcia's Planet* likely shared an orbit with the Earth around the sun. It also seems to indicate that it resided very near to Earth, perhaps nearly as close as the Moon. What made *Barcia's Planet* leave for its long orbits outside the solar system may have been the close passing of the large asteroid that killed off the dinosaurs 65 million years ago!

The wandering planet or perhaps the Earth's prodigal moon is a better descriptor, has a long and dangerous way to go to reach the orbit of Earth. It will have to pass through many hazards on its journey. But its predicted path is amazingly direct, the only question that seems to remain is, will it achieve a stable orbit around the sun, or blast off for another 2.5 million years? Hopefully, may the prodigal return home. What a boon to man that would be! Of course it may come so close as to be a threat to Earth itself."

"Aw jeez, there's always a fly in the ointment!" Someone remarked.

APRIL 30, 2049
BARSOOM STATION, MARS
PLANET DISCOVERY PLUS 11 DAYS

The next several days were hectic for the astronaut scientists of Barsoom Station. The observation of *Copernicus 13* now dubbed CP-13 for short, continued without interruption around the clock. Communication between the station and NASA increased exponentially as did coordination with the Europeans under Dr. Nigel St. John at the European Space Agency's Mars base, Darwin Station.

The Chinese Mars station team was scheduled to launch on their initial trip to the Red Planet just a few days after the monumental discovery of *Barcia's Planet.* Their mission was now on hold as they considered the ramifications of the American's startling find. They called for meetings with both NASA and the European Space Agency to consider what the future might hold.

Meanwhile, Doc divided the six astronauts into two teams to handle the additional workload. Only essential station life support tasks interrupted the new work schedule. Then, an impromptu meeting was called by Doc and held in the station headquarters area among the computers, readouts, and radar screens so work would not be interrupted too much.

Curiously, Doc and Hal spent many hours alone in the conference room for a number of days in quite consultation with NASA. It was unusual for such 'hush-hush' discussions and the exclusion of the other scientists, so naturally there was a good deal of pent up curiosity, and some resentment. Perhaps now they would find out why. Each of them gripped a cup of hot coffee or tea and looked expectantly at Doc.

"Hal has determined the distance to CP-13 from Mars and the speed of its approach has been determined as well as the angle of its approach. NASA has gone over and over our data and agrees with them. I know some of you, perhaps all of you, have felt kind of left out recently. I apologize for that, but now, I'll let Hal tell us all about it." Doc said.

Hal stood, and characteristically ran his hand over his shining bald head. This time he had the inevitable graphic presentation ready to roll. A screen appeared on the wall showing a simplistic graphic of a red Mars, white Phobos and Deimos, and off in one corner a small blue circle representing CP-13.

"CP-13 is traveling at a rate of speed that will put her close to Mars in a little over 8 Earth months. The approach speed of *Barcia's Planet* is just part of that equation, because Mars is hurtling in its orbit toward CP-13 as well. Add to that the fact that CP-13 is traveling uncharacteristically slow for a celestial body that at one time was ejected from the solar system at what must have been a tremendous speed. We have no idea why it has slowed down, perhaps an encounter with some as of now, unknown force in the depths of space. We just don't know, and here is where it gets sticky for us folks.

As *Barcia's Planet* passes by Mars it may cause planetary reactions."

Everyone looked around with an odd look on their faces. Then John said what was on all their minds. "What kind of planetary reactions are you talking about Dr. Boyle?" He asked in an exaggeratedly calm voice.

Hal hesitated and looked down at his graphic remote control device.

"We're not exactly sure what that means." Doc interjected. It could be Mars quakes, ground cracking pressures; the destruction of mountains, maybe even reawakened volcanic activity, although technically volcanism on Mars is dead. But we do know one thing for sure." He continued, and then looked at Hal. "You want to tell them?"

Hal nodded. "We do know it's going to be one hell of a show, something no human has ever witnessed." He paused again as if to catch his breath.

"As *Barcia's Planet* passes close to Mars it is going to rip first *Deimos*, and then *Phobos*, away." He held up his hand as four excited astronauts all tried to speak at once.

"Yes, CP-13 is going to steal the moons of Mars away and drag them along behind it!" Now everyone stared at him with open mouths. Again, it was John that spoke for the group.

"What the heck does that mean to us, and… and to Earth?" He gasped.

"We're just not sure John; we don't know what it will mean. But NASA wants us off the planet surface when it happens. We're to take the shuttle up and view the events as they happen. St. John's people will do likewise. Both stations will have their cameras and radars on, watching and recording everything that happens. Between them and us we will place seismic recorders as far away and in every direction from our stations as possible in the time we have, to get as much data as we can. There will be much more we have to do and I will outline that as we go along. But there is more folks; Hal has more amazing information for us." Doc continued.

Without a word Hal started the graphic film and they watched as the red circle of Mars moved toward the small blue circle of *Barcia's Planet* and the two smaller off-white circles of Deimos and Phobos continued to spin around Mars. The silence was complete as the blue circle closed in on and slid past the red circle, stripping away the two moons that dutifully fell in behind it.

Hal paused the video and turned back to them. "As a scientist I'm not sure I believe in the hand of providence. But that is all I have to explain what we have projected will happen next. Already traveling slow the stripping away of the moons of Mars by CP-13 and dragging them along behind will slow the wandering planet even more. It's hugely parabolic fall toward the sun will be shortened and made steeper. Exactly what trajectory it will then take is unknown. But our best guess puts it moving head-on toward Earth in what may become a cosmic game of billiards."

As Hal looked at the faces of his audience it was obvious they were shocked again. No one said anything, not even John, whose eyebrows were knitted together in a frown.

Trish's open face was flushed and she seemed to take small rapid breaths. As the discoverer and namesake of the wandering planet she couldn't help but feel some responsibility for the dangerously predicted and fantastically colossal events.

Rolf, his expression set in stone, eyes a hard icy blue, seemed to stare unblinkingly, his muscular arms folded protectively across his chest.

But Marjorie just seemed excited, her lips partly open, eyes shining as she straddled her desk chair backwards, arms akimbo on its back. "What a ride that's gonna be, hoo-ah!" She whispered, but loud enough for everyone to hear. Then, her excited expression still in place, she stared at Rolf a moment before turning back to Hal who resumed speaking.

"I know I'm getting repetitive, but we don't know what will happen as she approaches the inner circles of the Solar System. There may be collisions, there may not be. But we do know that as it stands right now... *Barcia's Planet* is headed for a probable solar orbit in the Goldilocks Zone, somewhere behind and likely closely following Earth. This may in fact, be the very position it occupied before being knocked out of orbit and flung into the far depths of space millions of years ago."

MAY 10, 2049
BARSOOM STATION, MARS
PLANET DISCOVERY PLUS 21 DAYS

"Five… four… Three… two… ignition and liftoff of Marathon Runner One!" John said as he pushed the firing button and sent the electrical charge surging to the rocket's igniter.

Inside the station Trish and Doc watched the small rocket as it seemingly leapt off the Martian ground riding the flame of its first stage as it ignited with a flash of oxygen and propellant. John and Marjorie were outside in their pressure suits situated behind the thick but completely clear launch shield a safe distance away. As the rocket sped upward Marjorie pumped her fist in the air and said "Hoo-ah, I love the sound of rockets in the morning!"

John grinned and nodded. "Reminds me of when my dad and I used to launch small rockets in a field near our house. I loved them then and I still love them now." He exclaimed.

Earlier the two astronauts used the rover's twin grasping arms to secure and move the twelve foot rocket to the launch pad. There they had fueled and oxygenated its holding tanks and connected it to the launch console via a number of umbilical cords.

Trish glanced at the other camera screen and noted Hal and Rolf standing on the shuttle's external electrical lift watching the launch. As the rocket disappeared leaving only its vapor trail, they returned to wrestling supplies and equipment through the cargo hold hatch for the crew's coming flight.

The rocket was one of three Marathon Runner surveillance craft at Barsoom Station. Its original mission was to survey the moons of Mars. Now, it was on its way to rendezvous with *Barcia's Planet* to give them their first up close and personal look at the wandering planet. They would soon follow up with a second launch, and finally a third set to follow along behind CP-13 after it slid by robbing Mars of its two satellites. The last rocket, after expending its fuel was to trail the planet and its two new moons to record the history making event. Since the crew would be off planet by then, the last launch command would be from space.

Exceedingly fast, Marathon Runner One would make radar contact with CP-13 in a matter of days. After the initial burst of speed from the chemical rockets of its first, second, and third stage, the rocket would rely on an ion thruster for the remainder of its journey. Half its time getting in orbit around the mysterious planet would entail deceleration.

Back in the station proper Trish followed Doc's gaze to what *Copernicus* was showing them. The planet's image was much larger now and a tinge of blue and smudge of what might be brown or red was faintly discernible beneath the ice. Doc leaned forward, squinting his eyes as he looked closer at the image. Trish looked again and then she saw what attracted his attention. "Is that what I think it is?" She asked.

Doc didn't reply for a moment, and then he nodded his head. "Well, yes, I think it is. It appears to be a haze around the edges of the planet. As if..." He started to say, his voice trailing off.

"As if it's got or is developing an atmosphere!" Trish said with a mixture of impatience and excitement. "But this far out Doc, and not all that warmed yet by the sun?"

Looking forward to a break for lunch inside the station in two hours, the launch team quickly mounted the rover and headed back to the inflated metal framed storage building. With Marjorie at the controls, the second rocket, Marathon Runner Two, was soon moved to the launch pad. They would wait twenty four hours before launching this surveillance probe, destined to take up a separate orbital station off *Barcia's Planet* and on the opposite side from the first rocket.

While the launch and guidance teams were working with the rocket, Hal and Rolf were inside the heavy lift ship *Astraeus* appropriately named for the Greek titan that controlled the stars and planets of the night sky. They were stocking the ship with all manner of supplies needed for a long voyage off-planet. The crew was uncertain how long they would have to be off of Mars or even if they would be able to return after the passing of *Barcia's Planet*. So they planned for the worst scenario.

During their breaks from the physical labor they checked the diagnostic program they were running on the systems of *Astraeus*. Things seemed to be progressing well.

While they awaited the rendezvous between the approaching planet and *Marathon Runner One*, the crew worked in shifts preparing the lift ship for eventual departure.

"I always hated moving day back home and I'm pretty sure I'll still hate it here on Mars!" John said.

"Yeah, and this time, after you load the truck up, you have to drive it too." Marjorie interjected and was pleased it elicited a few chuckles on the radio net.

"Hey guys," Doc said, transmitting on their work frequency. "I just thought you'd like to know that we've detected what appears to be a growing atmosphere on CP-13. I don't mean to steal Hal's thunder, but that is both a surprising and somewhat promising development. We'll keep a close eye on it and I'm sure Hal will have more information regarding it later on."

That evening, as the last red rays of the sun cast shadows across the darkening red sands, Doc stood looking out the observation window, his hands clasped behind his back as he rocked gently on his heels. Lost in his own thoughts he didn't hear Rolf approach until he spoke. "It's beautiful, is it not?"

Although a bit surprised, Doc quickly recovered and replied. "It most certainly is. I've begun to almost think of it as home."

"Yes that's true; even more so now that we will soon have to leave its relative safety for the unknown wonders, and dangers, of open space." Rolf continued.

"But think of the adventures set before us Rolf; we will be doing things and seeing things that no earthling has ever seen before." The distinctly feminine third voice of Marjorie joined in.

Doc looked over his shoulder a pleased smile crossing his face as he noted both Marjorie and Trish had joined them to look out the window. "Ah, the ladies have joined us Rolf." Doc said, now we must watch our language and put away the cigars." He continued, pantomiming he was blowing smoke.

"What's this, some kind of impromptu meeting of the minds?" John said, also arriving at the back of the growing crowd. "We'd better spread out, one errant meteor hitting the station could get us all!" He exclaimed with a smile.

"Easy Buck Rogers," Trish rejoined. "It's a big planet and meteors tend to be pretty small."

Doc turned around, his smile a little less evident now. He sensed some trepidation below the veil of humor displayed by his team. And he nodded as the last member, Hal, joined the group.

"I know things are pretty unsettled, it seems every day we find out new and puzzling and even somewhat scary information. We're looking at making an unscheduled space flight of unknown duration and to a degree, unknown mission coming up. But speaking for both myself and NASA I can tell you we have every confidence in each of you, in this team as a whole, and in the technology we have at our disposal.

Having said that, I cannot deny there is danger inherit in everything we do, our path is fraught with uncertainty and we not only have the weight of the world on our shoulders, but the weight of three worlds."

"Jeez Doc, what do you figure the odds are we're gonna survive these upcoming cosmic events?" John asked.

"Well, I think the odds are very good, we have a taut ship, good crew, and one of the finest pilots ever to don a spacesuit in the service of the Air Force and NASA. Now all we need are fair winds and full sails."

AUGUST 31, 2049
BARSOOM STATION, MARS
PLANET DISCOVERY PLUS 103 DAYS

There was so much to get done before the rendezvous between CP-13 and Mars that the time passed quickly. Daily and then hourly observations were made of the oncoming planet whose atmosphere continued to blossom like a rose in springtime. More details of the planet's surface became clear and the radar reports from the two Marathon probes showed mountains, valleys, hills, ravines and what was thought to be frozen lakes, one of which was so big as to be given the term "sea". Informally it was referred to as the Marathon Sea named for the probe that discovered it. One fly-over on the night side of the planet distinctly showed a fiery glow in at least one location. Volcanism was alive and well on CP-13.

The approach of the intruder planet created disturbances on the Martian surface as small tremors made the surface tremble awakening the ancient god of war from his long slumber. Soon Mars would indeed be at war, matching the strength of its gravity and hurtling speed against the greater swiftness and alien gravitational pull of *Barcia's Planet*. A true war of the worlds was fast approaching.

As the day of launch approached excitement arose among the crew, excitement that was matched at both NASA and ESA and the people of Earth. Everyone stayed glued to their video screens, mesmerized by the real life space drama.

As anyone who has ever left home for an undetermined time can attest, there are a thousand things to do before you actually leave. Turn off the lights, adjust the thermostat, water the plants, kennel the pets, and pack your clothing, equipment, emergency equipment, and supplies. Take those tasks and multiply them by another thousand and you have an idea of what the men and women of both the American and European observation stations had to do before they lifted off. But finally, launch day arrived.

Lieutenant Colonel John Cummings stood at the bottom of the retractable ramp, his hand resting on one of the stabilizing fins of the Heavy Lift Vehicle *Astraeus* (HLV – 16). She was the latest version of the space craft and sixteenth produced under the NASA contract with Boeing Rockwell Aerospace for a total production run of twenty space craft.

Other ships of the fleet serviced the U.S. moon bases, space stations in Earth orbit, and Barsoom Station. Two of the ships were dedicated to the recovery and recycling of the huge cloud of space debris circling Earth. The crews aboard them worked for commercial companies but were trained by NASA. The United Nations, although giving a nod to NASA's cleanup effort, had approached Boeing for a small fleet of five more HLVs to be manned by astronauts from many countries and to augment the debris recovery. The UN secretary general noted "Space debris threatens the people of Earth and the free use of space by all space faring nations."

John took a last look at Barsoom Station, he knew that when and if they returned, it might not even exist except as a pile of broken and deflated buildings and busted equipment. To limit damage they moved the rovers, generators, solar arrays and any other moveable pieces of equipment and supplies away from the buildings. Plastic tarps covered them and were secured to pins driven into bedrock by pneumatic drivers. As if to send him off, a Martian wind kicked up, pushing him in the back like an encouraging parent. With that urging he began walking up the ramp, his gaze lingering over the low yellow hills and red windswept sands of what he had come to regard as 'home'.

John entered the ship and pushed the button that started the ramp's retraction. As the portal closed automatic pumps pushed the Martian atmosphere outside where it belonged and when completed, filled the chamber with breathable air and the pressure of one Earth atmosphere. Despite that, John left his helmet in place as launch protocol dictated for all lift offs.

He made his way up the space craft's interior past the level where Rolf, Marjorie, and Trish were already strapped in. Almost in unison they turned to look at him, the lights glinting off their faceplates and he returned their waves and confident smiles as he passed.

Entering the upper level he clicked his ship/pilot commo button as he took a sip of water from the helmet siphon.

"Good morning Colonel Cummings". The ship computer greeted him in a feminine voice, following the military custom of usually addressing a lieutenant colonel with the higher rank title of colonel. "Good morning Linda, do you have a report for me?" He asked. As the first pilot of this spaceship he was given the right to name the ship's communication system. Linda, a pretty blonde, was his first girlfriend at the tender age of twelve. She had given him his first kiss on the lips by a female other than his mom.

"Yes I do John, all systems are nominal, and I am prepared for immediate launch upon your command." Linda continued.

"Very well Linda, stand by." He replied and then dialed into the ship-wide communication system and heard Doc, sitting beside him in the co-pilot chair speaking to Darwin Station.

"NASA will begin our countdown in approximately two minutes Captain Clark we will precede your launch by ten minutes to insure *Astraeus* is out of your way." Doc said and then paused.

"Roger Doctor O'Brian, ESA will begin our own countdown in about eight minutes and we will follow you up and into orbit. Good luck to you and the crew of *Astraeus*." Clark continued.

"John, NASA has given the one minute alert to launch". Linda said.

"Very well Linda, begin warm up procedures and retract the external antenna at launch sequence start." John replied.

"Thank you John". Linda replied and then lapsed into silence as NASA's transmission came to them, already eight minutes old. "T-minus 10, 9, 8…" the voice of launch control sounded in their helmets, then continued… 6, 5, and John felt the familiar butterflies he always experienced at launch 3, 2, 1 and ignition, liftoff, liftoff of HLV-16 the *Astraeus* on a historic mission to rendezvous with CP-13, better known now as *Barcia's Planet*! God speed *Astraeus!*" Even as launch control lapsed into silence the *Astraeus* sent its launch telemetry to them.

The rumble of their powerful engine, the descendant of those engines used in the famous Saturn 5 rockets, came clearly to them through the thin Martian air and entered their closed helmets.

"We have ignition John, the engine is operating nominally and will only have to use half of the thrust needed to escape Earth's gravity." Linda interjected as the ship eased off the ground in a smoothly accelerating climb. The crew was pushed back into their seats, but only gently as Mother Mars, as some of them had come to think of the Red Planet, willingly let them go with only a seeming tug of reluctance.

"Aw jeez, I never get over the thrill of liftoff." John said, his remark followed by a number of me too's from the rest of the crew.

John's eyes roved over the various sensor indicators with their green and yellow lights indicating the status of ship systems. His mind made a mental note that fuel would not appear to be a concern during the mission. He knew all too well the unexpected dangers that might arise during any kind of flight, even the routine ones.

Only the year before on a cloudless April morning John climbed into a T-6A Texan III at Vance Air Force Base in Oklahoma for a routine training flight. As an Air Force pilot he was required to log a set number of flight hours each month. This flight, as planned, would fulfill that month's requirement.

The T-6A Texan is a basic propeller driven airplane that allows a pilot to keep his standard flying skills up to date. Some might wonder how such a simple flying machine can keep the skills of a 21st century pilot more used to flying jets honed to a sharp edge. But regardless of the method of propulsion, propeller, jet, or rocket, the motor skills needed for flight remain the same.

John was alone, flying an *individual development sortie* to demonstrate his continuing proficiency. He took off almost effortlessly and flew a few patterns that included repeated landings and takeoffs from Vance, until he put his plane in a sharp right turn and headed up toward Kegelman Air Force Auxiliary Field near the Great Salt Plains in northern Oklahoma. He was flying a training mission the pilots dubbed "Dogface", perhaps an offhand tribute to the infantrymen of the U.S. Army, whose usual mode of travel was the exact opposite of the USAF.

John also performed a number of takeoffs and landings from Dogface and then piloted the single engine trainer to the military operations area or MOA situated twenty five air miles from Vance. MOA is an FAA area designated exclusively for military use. John intended to practice some tricky aerobatic maneuvers safely away from any other aircraft or people on the ground.

He was having a great time soaring, swooping, flying inverted, and steering his eager craft into sharp multiple g's producing turns that pressed him into his seat. It was so exhilarating he surpassed his usual "jeez..." for some joyous shouting. He swooped straight up into the blue skies until his plane stalled and toppled over to the left entering a spin as it headed toward the ground at breakneck speed. It was then his instruments showed his engine was having an oil pressure problem.

Bringing the plane out of the spin he saw that the oil pressure was fluctuating. Getting on the radio he declared an in-flight emergency and immediately climbed to 19 angels turning his aircraft back toward Vance.

John knew that his T-6A could glide two miles for every 1,000 feet of altitude and calculated he could make the base landing strip if the engine kept operating for just a few minutes more. But soon the pressure began to drop again and fell precipitously to zero. Through the silence left behind after the engine died John could hear the rush of wind past his canopy and the engine, blade still turning, begin to tear itself apart. John was now piloting a somewhat heavy glider.

Although he was in some degree of danger, John found the experience exciting and rather beautiful, there was now no sound except the passing air and occasional squawk of the radio as Vance tower tracked him, advising him of his altitude, angle of descent, and distance to the field. He quickly went through the procedures and prepared to fly an ELP or emergency landing pattern.

The goal was to be at 3,000 feet when his powerless aircraft flew over the airfield. If he could get to that position he could just basically roll his flaps and landing gear, letting the plane spiral down to land. And that is exactly what he did, demonstrating the cool, calm and deliberate actions and thought processes expected of pilots and astronauts. Little did he know he would soon need all those skills very soon. That evening he was the recipient of a number of toasts at the officer club. Soon after he had left Vance for Cape Canaveral passing the farewell sign as he exited the base main gate "Serve well, train hard, and return soon." A sentiment John hoped would come true.

Ten minutes into the historic flight, climbing higher and higher through the dust filled and perturbed atmosphere of Mars, the crew heard the European ship *Beagle* also lift off from the surface, now miles below and even more miles behind, the *Astraeus*.

Similar in nature to *Astraeus*, the European spaceship was built with an even greater lift capacity to accommodate its ten man crew, their equipment, and supplies. The gender mix of the ESA team was balanced equally with five men and five women, all single. But informal talking between the ladies during infrequent visits to one another's stations indicated some alliances existed, even if temporary in nature.

Like the *Astraeus*, the *Beagle* lifted easily from the surface of Mars and followed the lead ship, its speed slowly building to match. The two ships agreed in advance to take up positions where they could view their Mars bases except when the surface rotated out of sight, and also be able to view CP-13 as it advanced. Although *Copernicus* was earlier moved to a safe location, well away from the path of CP-13, it too could easily view and continue its analysis of the approaching planet.

Barcia's Planet was visible with the naked eye now and bore down relentlessly toward Mars and its two small moons. Some anxiety was evident aboard both spaceships and a lively conversation was carried on. They went about their assigned duties, with an air of expectation.

The adventure was fairly begun.

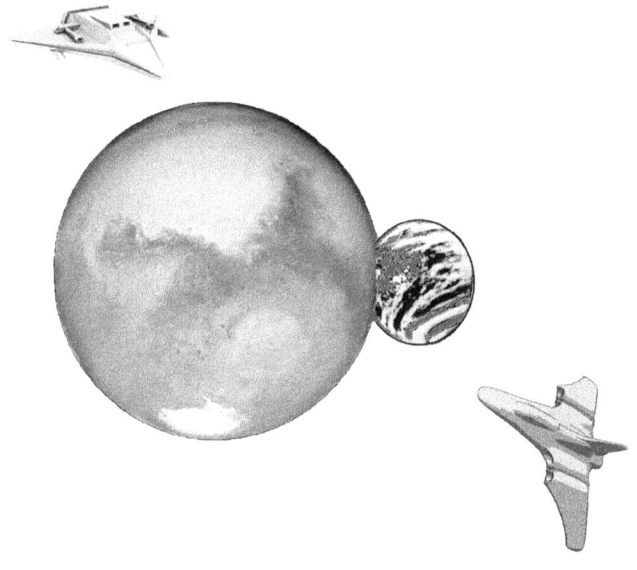

The view afforded the crew of the *Astraeus* upon assuming their designated position was spectacular and singular. Mars was spread out below them, with the twin white dots of its moons seeming to slide gently along its horizon. The stars were visible in their millions, spread across the void in a breathtaking panorama of immensity. The varying colors of the stars appeared as distant gems in the colors of red, blue, white, orange and yellow. But dominating and ominous in its approach was the varied white and blue orb of *Barcia's Planet*, looking like Earth's twin. It was such a contrast to the redness of Mars that it pulled the eyes of the crew away from their routine tasks of monitoring and observing over and over again. The tableau of the heavens was truly amazing and quite unique in the history of mankind.

"NASA's super computers have completed the analysis of CP-13's solar orbit. The distance is in the trillions of miles and even then it doesn't seem far enough. Nor would the gravity of the sun seem to be strong enough to keep *Barcia's Planet* from spinning off even deeper into the void, at least without help." Doc, who had removed his helmet and tore his eyes away from the approaching planet said, studying a tablet in his hand.

"In that case, how can it possibly return to the solar system, indeed even get close to the sun, on a regular basis?" Trish asked.

"Both ESA and NASA thinks that CP-13's long absence from the solar system may possibly be a confirmation of the existence of *Nemesis*." Doc continued.

"*Nemesis*, I thought that was only a myth, a legend, even perhaps, a fiction?" Marjorie interjected.

Hal replied. "It is all of that Marjorie and yet something more. *Nemesis* is postulated to be a brown dwarf star companion to Sol, orbiting the bigger star somewhere in the neighborhood of 1.5 light years away and somewhat outside the Oort Cloud. If it really exists, it could temporarily capture CP-13 and delay its return journey to Sol." Hal continued.

"That would suggest that *Barcia's Planet* is following an elliptical orbit. That it goes straight from Sol to the neighborhood of *Nemesis* and returns every two plus million years!" Rolf exclaimed. "Truly a mind boggling idea because it's not traveling fast enough to go the distance of one and a half light years!"

"That's why planetary scientists say that not only must *Nemesis* exist, but a wormhole too, that allows CP-13 to exit to the brown dwarf but also to reenter and return to Sol." Doc put in. "A big leap in logic and only a theory, but it explains what we see happening before our very eyes. I will say though that if *Nemesis* exists it is not detectable by infrared.

And that means that it has to be a cold brown dwarf, which is quite possible."

The eyes of the entire crew returned to CP-13, an interstellar truck possibly carrying a cargo of what? Was it bringing new minerals and elements, new chemistry and nuclear processes, perhaps even new life? Or did it harbor death and destruction of the Earth by impact or importation of deadly disease?

John, listening to the dialogue between the scientists now added.

"We may be on the brink of interstellar travel, even perhaps, the Interstellar Age! I say that because if there is a wormhole large enough and stable enough to allow the passage of an entire planet, it will allow the passage of star ships, even an entire armada of star ships!" No one disagreed with him.

"What's strange about the idea of *Nemesis* is that its existence was suggested way back in 1984 by paleontologists no less!" Trish offered, not yet ready to leave the subject. Before anyone could ask the question she continued.

"David Raup and Jack Sepkoski put forth the idea of *Nemesis* as an explanation for periodic mass extinctions of ancient flora and fauna on Earth. But at the same time astronomers Daniel Whitmire and

Albert Jackson also suggested *Nemesis* exists and resides in a highly elliptical orbit of Sol. Assuming CP-13 does come from the vicinity of *Nemesis* that would go a long way in explaining why it travels in an elliptical orbit. And as Rolf says, that indicates it travels at times in some unknown fashion, perhaps through a wormhole tunnel that allows a short cut through space."

The conversation gradually wound down to a murmur as the crew became more involved with observing various instruments, making notes in their computers, and watching the colossal events unfolding before them. They were truly viewing a war of the worlds.

John's gaze had never left the history making scene before them, a tableau that by now was on the screens of hundreds of millions of viewers back on Earth.

The *Beagle* was out of direct view as it assumed a position that placed her on the opposite side of Mars from the *Astraeus*. For her part the NASA ship was on the shadow side of the planet, well away from the path CP-13 would take as it sped by the Red Planet.

Barcia's Planet loomed large in the blackness of space and yet was still thousands of miles distant, rushing headlong at an enormous speed in excess of

40,000 miles per hour. The roaming planet's blue tinged sky, wrapped in grey and white clouds and illuminated in the distance-weakened light of Sol, bore an uncanny resemblance to mother Earth. So much so that subconsciously the crew's understandable anxiety at CP-13's approach softened and they began to see it as somewhat less of a threat. This view, premature in nature, was to quickly change in a surprisingly short period of time.

All data systems whether visual, radar, infrared or other types of sensors were pushed to the nth degree assembling, processing, and analyzing the flow of information arriving to them. The data was stored in memory for later perusal and use because it was impossible to keep up with it from minute to minute and even second to second. Data streams via radio were sent almost as soon as it was received back to Earth. Despite the speed of the instruments Trish was aware of a lag in time between real events and those displayed on their various screens. This was an anticipated phenomenon and she did not comment upon it.

Hours passed, but the crew did not grow tired, in fact they felt a renewed burst of energy as CP-13 drew closer and closer. A quick meal was eaten with sharpened appetites then they all settled back into their duty stations. Some of them wondered if their duty stations might turn into battle stations.

Deimos, the more distant of Mars' moons, was the first to feel the effects of the passing planet. CP-13's gravitational pull reached out and gripped the small rocky satellite, and it responded by following along, reluctantly at first and then with a rapidly growing acceleration. Trish spared a few moments of precious time to watch the tiny moon until the shadow of CP-13 overtook it and seemingly threw a dark cloak of invisibility around it. Glancing to see that it was still under surveillance of the sensors, she turned her view away and back toward Mars.

The Red Planet's growing anger at the approach of the intruder was fast becoming evident. Clouds of yellow and red dust rose and ballooned upwards, pushing past the normal limits of the thin atmosphere and jetted trails of planetary material into space, seemingly reaching towards *CP-13* like the deadly tentacles of an octopus. Exclamations of amazement came from the mesmerized crew as they pointed out new sights to one another.

John replied in the affirmative when a radio transmission arrived from the *Beagle* asking if they were seeing this awe inspiring event. Every human eye on the two ships and back home that could, was watching intently although separated in time and distance.

The approach of CP-13 caused some shift in the attitude of the ship, at first it was gentle and then increased in intensity. John's experience in shuttling between Earth and the moon as well as to and from the various orbiting space stations stood him in good stead. He skillfully used his small maneuvering rocket jets scattered around the exterior of *Astraeus* to keep the ship on station between the two converging planets and shifting moons. Distracted by John's maneuvering and the titanic gravitational battle of the planets, the crew sat in rapt silence. They all jumped in their space suits, including John, when the warning klaxon blasted out.

"Warning…warning… inbound debris vectoring from the dark side of CP-13." Linda's somewhat stilted voice announced. "Warning… inbound debris projected to strike the surface of Mars and may pose a danger to *Beagle*! No imminent danger to *Astraeus* detected at this time. This transmission is also being sent to the *Beagle,* warning… imminent arrival of debris to the last known position of the *Beagle.*"

Surprised like the rest of the crew John muttered, "Aw jeez!"

Minutes before, in the darkness of CP-13's shadow, the loosely held together nuggets of rock, sand, and ice that composed most of Deimos broke apart. Its weak gravity was no match for the growing surge and tug of the planet's gravitational pull. The denser pieces of the moon with their greater mass surged ahead of the disintegrating conglomeration of matter. As the rocks and boulders whip-sawed around CP-13, Mars' gravity also pulled on them and they accelerated in an ever increasing arc around the periphery of the planet.

The fragments sped around and down between the approaching planets and the tug from two directions spread them out like pellets shot from a shotgun.

The larger pieces succumbed to their mother planet's terminal call and peeled off, soon to impact the surface of Mars like so many Hiroshima sized atomic bombs.

The smaller chunks were again whip-sawed, this time around Mars and leapt, like greyhounds, down the gravity well tunnel between the two planets and on toward the nearly motionless and hapless *Beagle*!

John silently recalled what a carnival barker once said to him when he was a kid back in Texas, "It's like shooting fish in a barrel son, you just can't miss!"

Excited and flooded with adrenalin but managing to remain calm, John toggled ship to ship communications and said; "*Astraeus* to *Beagle*, meteor debris warning, probable impact on portside of *Beagle*. Take evasive action if possible, *Astraeus* engaging automatic laser cannon as targets bear."

As he spoke John's thumb selected and flipped up the red protective cap shield and toggled the target acquisition and fire button on the ship's joystick.

"Numerous bogies detected John, engaging." Linda said in her usual calm voice. As she completed her sentence the pod of laser cannons on each of the ship's three wings opened up, red energy bursts pulsed out in three continuous streams that flicked from one threatening boulder to another, ignoring the bigger objects headed not toward *Beagle* but toward the atmosphere of Mars. Lasers struck and vaporized or broke up the rocks into a quickly disbursing cloud of dust.

There had been no acknowledgement from *Beagle* but flickering laser fire from their quarter lanced around the other side of Mars to also engage the debris that was once Deimos. But there were more rocky missiles than the two spaceships could destroy and the crew of *Astraeus* watched them disappear arcing around Mars toward their friends and colleagues.

Linda's voice came back online and she said "Probable impact in 3...2...1 impact! *Beagle* emergency computer system confirms impact John."

"*Astraeus* to *Beagle*, can you report casualties and damages, over?" John asked.

"Do we have a visual on Phobos?" Doc asked as there was no immediate reply from *Beagle*.

A chorus of "Yes!" answered him, and then Marjorie said. "It's following along behind CP-13, maintaining its structural integrity and is projected to traverse to our front. Phobos appears to be a lapdog compared to Deimos. Deimos lived up to the meaning of its name, Dread!" She exclaimed.

The ship to ship radio crackled and then they heard a voice, taught with stress.

"*Beagle* to *Astraeus*, two dead, one injured, *Beagle* struck on the port bow and stern despite emergency use of maneuvering rockets. Our propulsion and navigation systems are damaged and offline. However, ship is currently maintaining hull integrity. We are, however, adrift in space."

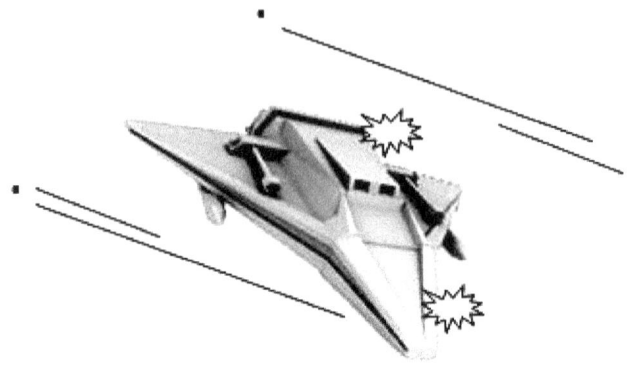

"Roger that *Beagle.*" John acknowledged. "We greatly regret the loss and injury of your people. Perhaps you can copy us on your report to ESA."

"Damn, I wonder who they lost." Doc said. "We got to know them pretty well during our Christmas visit to Darwin Station back in December." He continued. "They were and are our friends. We need to do what we can to help them out of this situation."

John who, along with Trish, was not yet on Mars when the first meeting of 'Martians' took place nodded in sympathy.

"Yes, I recommend we change station and move up to a polar view of the passing planets where we can still complete our observation mission and be much closer to the *Beagle.*" He said.

"Yes, I agree." Doc said and then relayed to the rest of the crew their intentions while John prepared to move *Astraeus* and contacted *Beagle* with the new plan.

"Seismic sensors on Mars are reading an increase of quakes in frequency, duration, and intensity. Recommend we launch the last Marathon. To delay could mean its destruction or at least inability to launch." Hal interjected.

"I agree with that, the larger pieces of Deimos will enter the atmosphere in under an hour." Rolf added. "They will detonate with extreme force and the trajectory places them landing near or on the area comprising Barsoom Station." He continued.

Doc gave the okay to Rolf's recommendation and relaxed just a little; the crew was obviously alert and performing their various tasks well, working effectively as a team.

"I'm launching Marathon Runner 3." Rolf said without any preliminary remarks or bothering with a countdown. "I'll follow its telemetry until it arrives off CP-13 and takes its orbital station."

Doc acknowledged Rolf stroking his chin in thought. "Hal, what do you see is likely to happen as CP-13 swings around Mars?"

Doc asked as John slowly accelerated the ship, the nose pointed up, relative to the two planets. The ignition of the engines came to them only as a vibration in the ship's hull. *Astraeus* responded almost effortlessly as it began to arc toward the pole of Mars. Capable of reaching speeds in excess of 40,000 miles per hour, she was a powerful ship.

"As *Barcia's Planet* comes smartly around Mars, the added gravitational pull of the Red Planet will add to her speed. Calculations indicate she will add approximately 5,000 miles per hour to her velocity as she comes out of the turn and accelerates toward Sol. With her present speed at a little over forty thousand mph, she will be very near the maximum speed of *Astraeus*." Hal paused a moment and then continued.

"I mention the speed factor because if Barsoom Station and possibly Darwin Station are both destroyed or damaged beyond use, we may have a real need for speed." He continued.

"Are you suggesting we may not be able to or want to return to Mars?" Marjorie interjected.

"I think he's right." John said, "Mars may possibly be taken off the table as an option if indeed the remnants of Deimos impact with the force we think they will. And if that's so..." He continued, trailing off.

"If that's so, we may be left with only two options, continue to Earth in the *Astraeus* and hope the *Beagle* can keep up, or land on CP-13 and construct a habitation there." Trish said.

"We'll know what options we have in just a moment. Sensors indicate the first Deimos debris impact just occurred." Rolf said his gaze going to his view screen, as did everyone else's.

The Martian night had fallen on the side of the planet where Barsoom Station was located. Suddenly there came a bright flash in the darkness and the crew gave a collective gasp because the size of the explosion was unexpected. It was soon followed by more flashes like heat lighting on a summer evening upon Earth. Some flashes were smaller than the first, some larger, but they continued for an extended duration of time and seemingly crowned the planet. Indeed the string of explosions continued around the circumference of the planet until they moved from night to the day side of the globe. The flashes continued, barely paled by the light of Sol and now they witnessed surging towers of mushroom clouds billowing up.

The destruction was massive in nature and left little doubt but that both stations were utterly destroyed in the death of the small moon. The slow rate of erosion on Mars, mostly confined to the wind, meant that the scars of Deimos' death would be evident for thousands of years if not eons.

Waxing poetic Rolf said "We have witnessed the fiery death of the war god's horse, or at least one of them, for Phobos yet lives."

"Amen." John said. "*Barcia's Planet* is not far behind and will be swinging around Mars soon. I propose we go help the *Beagle* and get her prepared to follow us to make landfall on CP-13."

He noted the hush that once again fell over the crew, who waited for Doc's confirmation that what John had said was what was going to happen.

Doc paused then said. "I see no other alternative; Mars is no longer suitable even for our isolated kind of occupation. Let's hope *Beagle* can affect repairs and join us. Otherwise..." He said, letting his voice trail away.

"Let's go see." John quipped, gripping the joystick and preparing the engines for restart. Across the top of Mars was the fastest route to the ESA spaceship and it didn't take long to spot the craft and gently edge up to it. "*Astraeus* to *Beagle*, situation report please." John said."

Dr. Nigel St. John replied quickly. "Some improvement *Astraeus*, the best we can figure is that we can likely produce about eighty percent of thrust. Our engineer officer was one of our casualties. However, I'm afraid our navigation is still out." He continued.

"Nigel, with the plan we want to propose navigation will likely not be much of an issue. But, we will need all the propulsion *Beagle* can muster." Doc replied.

"Go ahead with your proposal Daniel, we inferred the destruction of the two Mars stations although we couldn't see it, and so have likely come to the same solution you have. Please continue." Nigel said.

The two leaders of the science teams conferred, agreeing that landing on *Barcia's Planet* and riding it down to Sol was their only hope for survival. Nigel assured them that the food supplies aboard *Beagle* were undamaged and combined with those of *Astraeus* just might keep them alive until they could get some assistance from Earth.

"If Rolf's calculations are correct on the final speed of CP-13 toward Sol we could be there in less than six months. And if Earth were to launch a rescue mission with food and supplies the same time we land on CP-13, they could deliver them to us less than three months from now." Doc added.

"Well," Nigel replied. "I think our pilots need to confer on another channel and work out the details."

Doc nodded to John and he toggled his helmet com system to the previously agreed setting. "Hello Captain D'Artan, sorry we have to meet during such a tense situation."

"Yes, its rather unfortunate Colonel Cummings, but I am happy to get better acquainted with you none-the-less. Since time is short, shall we get right to the matter?" D'Artan said in a slight French accent that John was sure ladies found intriguing.

"I agree sir. To offset the increase of speed that *Barcia's Planet* will gain rounding Mars, we will follow its path as closely as possible. In that manner we will not only gain the push from Mars itself but may be able to pick up a little more speed from CP-13's gravitational pull as well. Operating that closely together may pose some risk, but it will minimize the need for your offline navigation systems." John said, pausing.

"Your proposed solution is the one we arrived at as well. I agree the navigation problems should be minimal, however, since we are as you say operating closely, perhaps your navigation computer can be digitally tied in to ours. In that manner, our two spaceships could maneuver as one." D'Artan said.

"I think that idea has merit Captain, I'll have to get our technicians to look at the proposal, but it sounds good. The big question is, how well do you think your engines will perform?" John said.

"I know my ship very well Colonel, and I believe the estimate of eighty-percent propulsion is perhaps a bit pessimistic. I know a few ways to, how you Americans say, 'tweak the system' for a bit more power at the necessary time, no?" D'Artan asked.

John had never seen the captain's face, but in his mind's eye he saw the Frenchman's mustache twitch in a smile. "Hell, he may not even have a mustache!" He thought to himself.

"I think we understand one another Captain, and I'm sure we both know our ships. Happy sailing, we will send the telemetry to you shortly. Goodbye my friend."

"Adieu, Colonel."

Connecting the two ships navigational systems didn't take long, and soon after that both ships were in position to watch *Barcia's Planet* make its final approach to Mars and then beyond it.

The two worlds appeared huge in the crew's view screens and through the observation ports of the ship's bridge. Despite its real position of several thousand miles on the opposite side of Mars, CP-13 loomed ominously over the Red Planet. The intruder planet seemed to move slowly as it began to pass behind Mars, pulling white and bright Phobos behind as though showing off its captive. The crews of both ships were stunned to see how much *Barcia's Planet* had changed, looking more and more like Earth itself.

The new world now showed blue seas with floating ice flows surrounding both islands and continents of land still covered in ice yet showing dark patches of soil.

Appropriately it was Trish who spoke in a dry emotional voice barely above a whisper but clearly audible to everyone in the spaceships. "My God, it…its home!"

AUGUST 31, 2049
INTERPLANETARY SPACE
PLANET DISCOVERY PLUS 103 DAYS

John was the first to come out of the awe inspired reverie. "Captain D'Artan, let's prepare to move out!"

"Aye, aye Colonel Cummings, the *Beagle* is prepared to follow *Astraeus*. Please forgive me when I say I perhaps feel a bit like La Salle when he chanced upon the mouth of the Mississippi River and envisioned a new world!" D'Artan replied.

The two ships smoothly accelerated in a wide arc that would bring them up behind both Phobos and CP-13. Now the ships accelerated in unison and were soon traveling at several thousands of miles per hour. Smoothly, John continued to pick up speed and gently began to bring the nose of *Astraeus* around and toward the white beacon that was Phobos.

Ahead of them CP-13 had now passed Mars, but had not escaped its gravitational tug that wrapped itself around the intruder planet as if it would wrest it from its headlong rush. In its turn *Barcia's Planet* reached out to embrace the Red Planet with its tendrils and arms of immense force of gravity.

73

Below, on the surface of Mars quakes rolled around the world of the god of war and the land appeared to writhe in torment.

"Rolf, begin Marathon 3's final run." Doc said. Feed the images and data directly to John and Captain D'Artan."

"Very well!" Rolf exclaimed, his fingers flying across his intuitive control board. "Phobos is coming into view." He continued.

John looked down to see that it was so. The probe was skimming above the moon, showing its rocky surface replete with craters, craggy hills and mountains interspersed with smooth open plains. Like Earth's moon there were darker patched flows, evidence of a geologically active past.

"Trish, your planet is not only like Earth, but now it has a moon very similar to Earth's. It's uncanny." John said and pushed the speed forward almost to the stops.

Astraeus leapt ahead as the crew were pushed deeper into their seats. Ahead of them CP-13 was past Mars and telemetry readings indicated that it was starting to make its turn, a turn that would point it toward Sol. But somewhere in the back of his mind John realized, that it was also turning toward Earth.

Ignoring the sense of foreboding that came over him, John heeled the ship hard to the starboard vectoring in on Phobos. His speed readout indicated the ship was approaching thirty-six thousand miles an hour, threshold of the *Beagle's* projected terminal velocity. Glancing at his radar John was relieved to see the ESA ship was maintaining station. But he knew the final test was coming soon.

The gravity of Mars was once again pulling on the *Astraeus* adding its slingshot effect to the ship's already great speed. And that was a good thing because *Barcia's Planet* was already accelerating away from them. John was not concerned about the *Beagle's* speed because at this point both ships were speeding equally under the Red Planet's influence.

Phobos, a smaller mass than CP-13 and of course not fitted out with engines was not surging ahead as fast. The ship now overtook the newly captured moon and everyone got a firsthand view of the kidnapped satellite as they flashed by, skimming overhead. The only target in front of them now was the intruder planet, CP-13.

An hour after passing Phobos the gravity of *Barcia's Planet* began to have an effect, but John could tell it was not going to be enough. If they were unable to increase speed they would bounce off the planet's outer atmosphere and not be able to push past the threshold. "Aw jeez, here we go!" John thought.

Reaching out he toggled the com to *Beagle*. "Captain D'Artan, are you with me, are you ready?" He asked.

"Affirmative Colonel, we are standing by for full throttle." D'Artan responded.

"Follow my lead!" John said as he pushed the speed control literally to the stops and watched his indicator.

"Request vocal readout on speed Linda relative to CP-13 for both *Astraeus* and *Beagle* please." John said.

"Very well John, CP-13 is moving away from both ships at 46.49 thousand mph. *Astraeus* is following 45.2 thousand mph while *Beagle* is at 42.9 thousand mph. I project that the planet's pull will increase both ships speed by 3 percent an hour. *Astraeus* will attain the atmosphere penetration velocity of 46.76 in approximately one hour. *Beagle* will attain a final velocity of 44.19 thousand mph, insufficient to attain atmospheric penetration."

"D'Artan, you need more speed, pour the coals to her Jacque, give her the whip!" John cried.

"Ah, I am afraid she is at the utmost now my Colonel. She is, uh, how you Americans say 'tapped out." D'Artan replied.

"You can't get any more out of her D'Artan? Look again, you just need a little more speed to reach atmosphere penetration, we're almost home free man!" John said, louder than was necessary.

"John, I can perhaps get more speed, but the damage to the exhaust cone is causing turbulence and massive vibrations to the hull, I am afraid *Beagle* may shake herself apart!" D'Artan said emotionally, the first indication that he thought the crew on *Beagle* were all going to die.

"*Astraeus* is now at 46.7 thousand miles per hour and overtaking CP-13. *Beagle* remains at 42.9 thousand mph and will fail penetration of atmosphere in 9 minutes 23 seconds." Linda said.

"Listen Captain, if you don't get your ship speed up *Beagle* will fail, you will fall away and have to try to make it to Earth just with your ship. You might make it, who knows? If you can push her just a bit more you can land on a near Earth planet and help us survive too. We need you guys with us Jacque, you said you could tweak her, do it now!" John yelled.

There was no answer from the *Beagle* and minutes passed. John slumped in his chair and glanced at Doc shaking his head.

"Penetration of atmosphere in two minutes." Linda said and paused. "*Beagle's* speed has increased to 43.5 thousand mph, 44.2 mph and climbing, 45.8 mph...*Beagle* has successfully attained atmospheric penetration velocity." Linda announced unemotionally.

But the crew was cheering and John toggled ship to ship commo and said "Hear that *Beagle*? I knew you could do it Jacque, I couldn't have done it with your ship, but you could, you know how to tweak her!"

A gentle warning klaxon sounded. "Atmospheric penetration achieved, automatic rotation and retro firing, prepare for drogue chute deployment." Linda said.

"The landing site selected is on the main continent of *Barcia's Planet* as indicated by data from the three Marathon probes. The site is a relatively open and smooth plain with close access to a source of water. Landing will be accomplished in 21.6 minutes from my tone." This announcement by Linda was followed with a gentle tone.

All the crew could see was the stars above them with a now more distant view of Mars, their former home. They all burst into conversation and no one switched the cameras to view the upcoming surface of *Barcia's Planet* for a number of minutes. And that is when they got their first close-up view of their home for the next six months.

The plain they were descending to was a mosaic of tans, browns, and whites where soil or at least what they took it to be soil, showed through the ice. Six minutes later with a roar of engines and a gentle bump, *Astraeus* landed.

In the deafening silence they heard the distant sound of a rocket engine firing and then silence again. The *Beagle* had landed. Man had reached their home away from home.

SEPTEMBER 1, 2049
PLANETARY ARRIVAL PLUS 0 DAYS
BARCIA'S PLANET

Everyone admitted they were tired, everyone admitted they were too excited to sleep. The Earth ships landed on the planet's surface in what appeared to be late afternoon. Looking through the ship portholes they could see that the sun shined weakly through a blue tinged atmosphere and wispy white clouds. Although it was day, the blackness of space hovered in the background and the stars were quite visible. The landscape was made up mostly of ice, and as they watched, a snow shower quickly passed across the plain.

"Hot damn, I want to drink wine and go for a nice long walk!" Marjorie said, standing up from her seat, removing her helmet, and stretching.

"Well, if you want to drink wine you'll have to do it in the ship because if you go for a walk you'll have to remain suited up." Hal said.

"Oxygen is present, but not yet at a high enough pressure for us to breath. The gravity here on *Barcia* is only a little more than two-thirds that of Earth, so the walking part is easier anyway."

"That means instead of a hundred and twenty pounds of loveliness I only weigh in at eighty pounds or so, hoo ah!" Marjorie responded.

"Actually gang, if you don't want to sleep we need to get out on the surface and start stuffing things in specimen jars for analysis. We need to know what makes this rock tick and we need to know it soon." Doc said, heading for the airlock. "Let's go."

The others got up to follow while Marjorie excitedly put her helmet back on. Each of them picked up a specimen sampling kit that was a little more complicated than just collecting jars.

With Trish standing next to him Doc cycled the airlock system and when the ready light turned green, rotated the handle and opened the gangway hatch. He was reaching for the hydraulic lever when Trish put her hand on his arm. "Look". She said.

All of them paused and then crowded up to see what Trish and Doc were looking at. The scene took their breath away. Mars was still very close and filled a good portion of the sky. Viewed from the portholes the clouds hid the Red Planet from view. Now it was displayed in all its glory, the tan, light brown and red sands of the surface, stirred by the explosive debris of Deimos, created a bright orange world. It resembled nothing so much as a pumpkin, and since it was indeed October, it was very appropriate. They stood silently looking for a few moments, undistracted until John spoke.

"It's beautiful, but it also looks…wrong, like something is out of place." He said.

"And something is, isn't it Hal?" Rolf asked, turning to look at the planetary scientist.

"It is indeed Rolf. Without the stabilizing influence of its moons, Mars is shifting on its axis. The northern pole is rotating to expose itself to direct sunlight. And later, it may flip flop again. I'm afraid that CP-13 has wreaked terrible damage on our old home." Hal continued, and some of them swore later they heard a catch in his voice.

"Think about it." Rolf continued, "We were once Martians and now, we're what...Barcians?" He asked, in what came close to being a joke.

"Wow Trish, he's right!" Marjorie exclaimed, "We are Barcians!"

Pulling the lever that started the hydraulic ramp's descent to the planet Doc said. "Well, come on Barcians, we got a planet to explore!"

They trooped down toward the ground behind Doc who paused at the last step and with Rolf filming it, placed his foot, the first human foot to step on *Barcia's Planet* firmly on an ice free patch of soil.

"I am truly humble..." he said, "...to join the ranks of such space explorers as Neil Armstrong on the moon and Amelia Anderson on Mars as I make this first step upon *Barcia's Planet.*"

The other four astronauts besides Rolf who was still filming gave a round of applause.

"This is not the act of one man, but of a dedicated team of space explorers; Dr. Trish Barcia who as all school children know by now, discovered *Barcia's*

Planet. Doctors Hal Boyle, Rolf Earhart, Marjorie Fox and Colonel John Cummings without whom this day would not have arrived. Thank you."

As Rolf shut down the camera Hal said. "Let's get that sent out as soon as possible Rolf and make sure the time and date stamp is correct."

All six of the astronauts now spread out and began to look around the familiar and yet alien landscape. The plain was in a bowl-shaped depression that rose a few feet upward from their position and then terminated in some steep foothills. Beyond the foothills rose a line of boulder-strewn and midsized mountains that stood out starkly with their jagged points jutting into the sky. They completely surrounded the plain except for an opening to the west. Every once in awhile a dark plume of smoke could be seen rising from among the mountains.

The plain itself was somewhat smooth with an occasional pile of stones. Patches of soil with some variation in color from dark brown to tan showed through the ice and snow. An almost eerie mist rose from just about everywhere for a couple of feet before dissipating. The sun was moving toward the western opening and just like on Earth, the clouds were turning red and yellow. In the distance a body of water shimmered golden reflecting the setting sun.

"Chalk up another similarity to Earth, *Barcia* rotates east to west, just like home." John said, doing what humans often do, shortening a phrase like *Barcia's Planet* to simply *Barcia*.

"Aw, leave it up to you John to look on such a beautiful sight and make a very romantic observation." Marjorie joked.

Hearing the unmistakable sound of hydraulics whining the group turned and saw a ramp lowering from beneath *Beagle*. A number of astronauts came down the walkway which was situated at such an angle that the Americans could only see the ramp's underside, their view of the other group restricted mainly to their backs from the waist down. But the group's leader was some way out in front of them and could be seen raising a tablet and reading out load from it. The distance was such that all they could hear was a murmur of speech.

"Hmm, looks like our Euro friends were also prepared for the whole first step thing." Trish said as the leading figure, assumed to be Dr. St. John, stepped sideways and waved conspicuously at them. They all returned the greeting and watched in some surprise as the ESA crew trooped back up the ramp and into their ship.

Kicking back some of the snow and ice from the surface, Marjorie squatted down and picked up a handful of the dark soil. For some reason the others stopped to watch her. She put soil into a specimen container and sealed it, then took another handful and kneaded it in her glove, stirred it with the index finger of her other hand, and slowly allowed it to fall back to the surface.

"I can't feel or smell this dirt, but it looks and acts like nothing less than the rich farm soil of my native Oklahoma." She said, standing back up.

"As much as I could wish it were so Marjorie, it's more than likely sterile with no bacteria, no worms and no grubs or any other type of life form." Hal said.

Marjorie turned and looked Hal in the eye, and if a woman wearing a helmet can jut out her chin, she did. "I think you may very well be wrong Dr. Halberd Boyle, until I know otherwise I believe the soil on this planet is viable for life." She said.

Even through the visor of his helmet Hal was seen to blush. No one on the team even after all the time they had spent together on Mars, had ever addressed him by his entire first name.

Doc stepped between the two of them. "We haven't done any scientific analysis and until we do, anything is possible." He paused for effect and turned his head to scan the plain. "There is something about this planet, something very familiar and yet, not." He said.

"Ah, jeez!" John interrupted. "Take a look at the ESA ship."

The group of European astronauts were coming down the ramp again, this time carrying a body bag, followed by another and then another.

"Ah, that explains why they went back aboard so quickly." Doc said, "Secure your equipment, and come with me." He continued, turning and walking deliberately toward *Beagle.*

It only took a few short minutes to trudge the hundred yards or so to the other ship. Dr. St. John walked out to meet them, and by the time they arrived, the body bags were laid out in a neat row. The astronauts of *Beagle* were gathered and the Americans fell in line with them, making a horseshoe circle with Dr. St. John standing apart.

"Welcome *Astraeus.*" Nigel said, using the traditional navy greeting, assigning the name of a ship to her commander and crew.

"We gather on this auspicious day for mankind to pause in our endeavors and say goodbye to our friends. These three explorers lost their lives in the service of the European Union and by extension, all the People of Earth. Here, in this place of perpetual memory we lay to rest Dr. Louis Galileo D'Angello, Dr. Willem VanVenter, and Lieutenant Commander Juan Castro Desilva."

The service went on, and when the speech was over the Americans joined in to help dig the graves, chipping the upper ice and snow away and laboriously digging into the frozen subsoil. By the time they had spread the last shovel full of dirt in the last grave the sun was dipping into the sea, and the sky lit up with one last burst of color. Everyone agreed it was a beautiful ceremony.

Markers consisting of three foot metal building fasteners were driven into the ground to mark the graves. And after a brief gathering and agreement to meet at first light, the two exhausted teams left for their respective ships and some well deserved rest.

But on the way back, John stopped to climb a low pile of rocks and took a long look back at Mars. He wasn't too surprised when Marjorie joined him. It was after all, a magnificent sight.

Looking at the beauty of devastated Mars and talking in low murmurs, neither of them noted the furtive movement among the rocks behind them and to their right.

SEPTEMBER 6, 2049
PLANETARY ARRIVAL PLUS 5 DAYS
BARCIA'S PLANET

Hal was the oldest crew member, the senior astronaut and the only scientist whose specialty was planetary science. Doc put him to work doing the first explorations and analysis. The rest of the crew including himself joined the Europeans in planning the layout and construction of Joint Station Alpha.

The station would house all the Earth astronauts with a men's dorm and a women's dorm. This would be a lot different than the individual rooms they enjoyed on Mars. But inflatable reinforced building modules were in short supply. Both NASA and the ESA however had coordinated before their respective Mars missions and insured that the modules of each space team were compatible with one another. In addition to the dorms there were separate labs for processing different kinds of specimens such as geological and others, if there proved to be "others".

Still a bit miffed about Marjorie's irritating remarks to him, Hal first began to analyze the soil samples. Taking melt water from the planet's ice he mixed it with the soil in a closed tube system and attached sensors to collect and process any resulting gases. Not that he expected any.

Then, donning his suit he went outside and paused for a moment taking in his surroundings. The mist was still rising from the planet's surface, and Hal expected that to continue for an indefinite time. The sun was up, doing its best to join *Barcia's* internal geological warming system to bring the planet's temperature up. It was already above freezing at a balmy 34 degrees.

In addition to finding the warming system Hal determined that the planet possessed a strong magnetic field, vital in keeping the charged particles of the Solar wind from ripping away its atmosphere. It then followed that the intruder planet also had magnetic poles, and it really came as no surprise to him when Hal pulled the compass from his hip pack and watched it point, north. He nodded, everything on the planet pointed to the fact that it was cast from the very same materials as the other four rocky planets of the Solar System; Mercury, Venus, Mars, and of course Earth.

He turned from his thoughts for a moment and watched the combined astronauts busily working together to build the station. Some were moving supplies and materials while others were connecting supports and stretching airtight fabrics that would later harden in place. Others were assembling power generators and laying heavily protected wiring. He smiled, they would have this place put up in no time. Later, soil and stones stacked and methodically piled against the walls and then solidified with cement like adhesive would provide even more protection.

Hal stepped off and headed toward a small overhead shelter, similar to a carport, constructed temporarily to keep the occasional snow and rain shower off equipment. Inside he climbed into a small earth moving machine only slightly bigger than himself with a bucket loader in front.

If the machine had an internal combustion engine Hal thought it just might find enough oxygen in the air to start up. But it was all electric and as robust and strong as any earth mover on Earth.

Hal toggled his helmet radio and contacted Doc. "I'm headed out toward the nearest foothill and see if I can find some interesting rocks. By the way, compasses work here just like back home. They point to the north."

"Roger that Hal, please stay in sight of the base because you are on your own. I'm gonna assign a couple of people to keep an eye on your progress.

Give us a call if you need anything." Doc said, and then signed off.

Hal set off, he was in his element, moving across land and looking to see what he could find, a geologist's and certainly a planetary scientist's dream come true.

The tracked vehicle easily moved across the tundra heading north toward the foothills. Along the way he stopped a number of times to pickup rocks native to *Barcia* as well as a surprising number of meteorites. Mostly black in color, they absorbed the heat of the sunlight and melted the snow off their surface making them easily visible.

Hal grew fatigued from the nearly constant stopping and climbing in and out of the dirt mover. He paused and surveyed his surroundings. In the distance he could see one of the dark smoke columns reaching upward toward the ever present clouds. Light snow and rain seemingly followed his progress across the snowy plains. A sound of gurgling water came to him and he noted several small rivulets of melt water flowing off the hills.

It appeared to him there were more patches of ice-free soil than yesterday and as his gaze swept over the closest hillside he paused. Something had caught his eye, what was it? And then he saw it again, an outcropping of bluish-grey rock that stood out from the snow covered soil around it.

Walking over he brushed the snow aside and leaning over the embankment and balancing on one hand, he took a closer look. He caught his breath, was he seeing what he thought he was seeing? Was it possible? He tugged at the rock, but it was bigger and thicker than it looked and ran back under the dirt.

Standing up Hal returned to the dirt mover, his eye passing over but his brain not registering the gray-green algae-looking patch on the back of the rock.

Reaching into the small truck bed on the back he picked up his rock hammer and returned. A couple of well placed whacks with the hammer and he was rewarded with an eight by five inch sample. He brought the sample close to his helmet visor and despite the fact that it was almost noon, flipped on his external helmet light.

His eyes widened in amazement, there was no mistaking the igneous rock with its large grain, blue and blue-grey appearance. He was holding the Genesis Rock in his hand. This formation of stone was actually laid down four billion years in the past, during the formation of the Solar System. It was only known to exist on Earth, Earth's moon, and now on *Barcia*!

Hal's churning thoughts were interrupted by the radio. "Hal, Doc here, commo check." The interruption jolted the planetary scientist back to reality.

"Hello Doc, I read you five by five." Hal said, indicating the transmission was loud and clear.

"Your O2 sensor is likely about to ping you, time to come home." Doc said.

"Uh yeah, yeah…" Doc replied distractedly just before the sensor did indeed ping and a mechanical sounding voice said "Warning, air pressure low…warning, air pressure low". "I'm headed your way now. I picked up some interesting rocks today." Hal continued.

"That's great Hal see you in a half hour." Doc replied.

"Shoot, it was way back in September of 2015 that NASA announced they were convinced there was free flowing water on Mars. You remember how they referred to it?" Marjorie asked.

The crew was back inside *Astraeus* after the long day of working on the new station. Joining them and the recipient of Marjorie's question was Lady

Janet Warner, a member of the ESA team and the subject of King William V. And as John would readily attest, a beautiful blonde lady whose figure, presently obscured by her spacesuit, was no doubt just as engaging as her looks.

"Indeed I do." Janet said. "I think every student in Great Britain knows the phrase 'Recurring slope lineae' or RSL as NASA chose to dub it." She continued.

"Yes, what an obscure reference, that basically meant lines of water flowing downhill! And it was only twenty years later in 2035 that life, in the form of microbes was found to exist on Mars! And here we are fourteen years later standing on a planet that is brim full of water. There just cannot be any doubt but that we will find life on *Barcia*!" Marjorie continued.

"We took a number of soil and water samples and are cooking them up in the lab to see if we come up with any bacteria or other kinds of microbes." Janet continued.

While other crewmen went about routine shipboard tasks John sat patiently, hanging on every word spoken by the two women, especially Janet, whose light blue eyes turned toward him now and then. Unnoticed Doc watched him and smiled. It was hard to get a word in edgewise.

"We've done the very same thing." Marjorie continued. "Hal set some experiments up before he went off exploring alone, I might add." Marjorie said looking at Doc. She had quietly questioned Doc on the advisability of allowing Hal to do that.

At the mention of Hal Doc straightened up and looked at his watch. "Speaking of Hal, he should have been back five or ten minutes ago." He said. "I'll raise him on the radio for a commo check."

But repeated calls by Doc were only met with silence. He glanced around at the looks of growing concern.

"Let's go, John you're with me!" He said.

The others all protested they wanted to go too but Doc held up his hand as he and John stepped into the airlock.

"No, we'll take an oxygen tank with us, the two of us even without a rover can get this done. The rest of you wait here!"

Doc said in a commanding voice that they knew would brook no argument, or would it?

When Doc and John stepped out of the air lock they immediately looked in the direction Hal had gone. Sure enough they could see the rover about one hundred yards away. The front of the vehicle was facing them but there was no sign of Hal.

As they started hurriedly down the ramp Trish joined them. Doc looked back at her but didn't stop and said "What are you doing Trish I told you the two of us can handle this."

"I'm the designated flight surgeon Doc and my duty is to attend all medical emergencies." She replied following them as they began jogging across the ice and snow covered plain. Doc merely grunted in answer and they moved as rapidly as their cumbersome spacesuits allowed. About a third of the way there Doc stumbled and fell, spread eagled on the ground. "Go on!" He croaked. "I'll catch up."

Moments later, moments that seemed an eternity, John and Trish reached the dirt mover. There, lying behind the tracked vehicle lay Hal. He was not moving and didn't respond either to their touch or their verbal inquiries. A mechanical voice was sounding in his helmet "…warning, air pressure less than twenty percent…warning, air pressure less than twenty percent…".

"His visor is open!" John blurted. "He's unconscious and breathing the atmosphere!"

"Hook up the oxygen tank he's inhaling the equivalent of thin air at the top of Mount Everest!" Trish exclaimed. "Of course if we were still on Mars he'd be dead by now!"

Reaching behind Hal's helmet John hooked the tank up to the emergency air system intake. This additional system eliminated the time consuming task of unhooking the suit's internal air system. John cracked the valve open as Trish leaned over to listen for the hiss of air into Hal's suit. Satisfied at what she heard she snapped his visor closed just as Doc breathlessly arrived.

"How is he?" Doc asked, squatting down next to his unmoving friend to look inside his helmet.

"He's still alive Doc, but will likely suffer the effects of oxygen deprivation. How serious those effects will be is hard to know. He's been breathing some very thin air." Trish said.

"And, he's contaminated Doc with any virus or bacteria that may thrive on *Barcia*." John added.

Doc nodded knowingly. "Well it was a near run thing and it may not be over." He said.

SEPTEMBER 10, 2049
PLANETARY ARRIVAL PLUS 11 DAYS
BARCIA'S PLANET

With many chores of her own to attend to, it was four days after Hal's injury before Marjorie entered his lab. Almost immediately she noticed the glass flask of moist soil with a gas spectrometer attached to it. Spotting Hal's notebook beside the flask she picked it up and read the notations hastily scribbled in his slanted hand. 'Sep 6, 2049 initiated microbe testing of Barcian soil using a soil fumigation method. I added chloroform in flask A while flask B remains as the control.' That simple phrase was the entire entry.

Marjorie tossed her hair back out of her eyes and gazed at the wall for a moment, thinking. She was familiar with the test, but she hesitated to interfere in another scientist's experiment. However, she was curious and it might be some time before Hal was back up. She flinched at the idea that if there were microbes, the chloroform had killed them, at least the ones, if any, in flask A. Meet interesting Barcians and kill them. Her mind made up, she took the next steps of the experiment noting each procedure in Hal's note book.

The first thing she did was to introduce cytoplasm into both flasks waited the required time and then extracted the carbon emissions of each one.

She then placed the carbon into test tube like condensing towers for analysis. Scanning the results with an infrared reader showed carbon was present in both flasks of soil. This was a positive indication of microbial life, but Marjorie wanted a more definitive result.

She now extracted soil from the two flasks to scan them under the electron microscope. Using biohazard elimination procedures, she was careful not to expose the soil or its possible microbes to the ship's environment.

There, in the fumigated soil she found dead microbes, microbes that looked no different to her than those found in Earth soil. She then took the soil from the control flask and scanned it. The results were the same except she found live microbes!

Marjorie caught her breath in surprise and with some satisfaction in the vindication that her tossed off remark to Hal about the soil being alive was true. For there, right before her eyes was evidence that the dirt of *Barcia's Planet* supported life, that it contained microscopic life!

"Yahoooo!" She cried, "Barcia's Planet has life!" And back to her from other crew members came exclamations of... "What, what did you say!" "Life!? On *Barcia*?"

It wasn't long before the entire crew was in the lab cubicle or in the hallway outside the cubical and everyone was talking at once.

"Okay, hold on gang." Doc said and then turned to Marjorie. "Don't misunderstand me Marjorie when I say...are you sure? Are you sure there was no contamination from us in the samples you tested?" He said, looking earnestly into her eyes.

"I'm pretty sure Doc. Hal started the experiments before his injury, but his notes indicate he followed procedure." She said.

Doc nodded then said. "Well, he's still unconscious and since we can't ask him. I'm going to ask you to do the tests again and with one of the others helping and observing. This is too important to be wrong about Marjorie. It's wonderful news and means a great deal to the future of humans on this planet, so let's get it right."

Marjorie paused a moment and then smiled. "Yes, of course, that is the right way to confirm this.

Doc smiled too and turned to the crew. "Keep this information to ourselves until we have time to confirm it. And that means we don't discuss this with our European friends either." Doc continued.

Everyone murmured their agreement, but they also congratulated Marjorie on her findings. They knew that this kind of thing could make a scientist's career and bring recognition from on high. Or, if the findings were wrong it could also ruin a career and bring ridicule for life.

SEPTEMBER 16, 2049
PLANETARY ARRIVAL PLUS 17 DAYS
NASA HEADQUARTERS, EARTH

The director of NASA, Dr. Hans Russell, better known by his nickname of 'Hank' sat at his desk pouring over the latest reports from Joint Station Alpha. What he was reading was truly astonishing and full of promise for the future. He had only briefly watched one of the many films of the near collision of Mars and *Barcia's Planet*. His chief of staff Lowell Black described them as 'nearly overwhelming' and stated the view was 'heretofore, only privy to the gods'. Hank looked at him with his head cocked and said, "The gods Lowell?" Black replied it was only a figure of speech. But Hank understood what he meant.

Hank moved on to the paper on *Barcia's* probable orbit following its whip-turn around Mars and the subsequent boost to its acceleration. The optimistic estimate showed the wandering planet taking up a solar orbit in the habitable zone a few thousand miles inside that of Earth's. And even better, it showed its final location, after orbiting for a few short years, about two thirds of the way around the sun from Earth's position. He really wanted them to look at this estimate again and go through it step by step with him.

Laying the report aside, Hank leaned back in his desk chair and watched the holographic display play out on the front edge of his desk. Filmed a few years in the past, it showed him playing three cornered catch with his son Justin and his daughter Ronnie, short for Veronica, with his wife Carol standing in the background laughing and clapping the sun reflecting in her golden hair. He had the sound off, but when it was on, he was back nearly ten years ago in that park with them all.

A knock sounded on his office door and Lowell stuck his head inside and said "Sorry chief, Director Stanford wants a word with you, he says its urgent." He said as Stanford stepped around him.

Turning off the hologram Hank stood up, buttoning the first button on his blue sport coat. He was wearing khaki slacks with a white shirt and a tie with red dominating in its mix of colors. A small white, blue, and red NASA pin on his left lapel completed his look of professional yet relaxed attire.

The NASA director stood over six feet tall and despite pushing fifty rather hard, he was still slim. Clean shaven except for a dark brush cut mustache that he was told more than once, made him look like a long past actor of some popularity named Tom Selleck.

He had dark brown hair, so dark in fact that it looked almost black, without a speck of gray to mar its sheen. His eyes were deep blue, the legacy of his maternal grandfather who was of Prussian descent. His first name was the second part of Grandpa Hans' legacy to him. Hank had a strong jaw line and a jutting chin marred by a white scar he'd gotten years before during his military service as an officer in the Air Force.

"Hello George, what brings you all the way out here from D.C.?" Hank said, extending his hand in greeting.

"Thanks for seeing me without any advance notice." George Stanford said in a soft voice, taking Hank's hand in a firm grip.

Hank was pleased, he hated to shake hands with someone who returned his own solid grip with a limp, what he called 'dead fish' handshake. Hank dismissed Lowell with a wave of thanks and surveyed the man before him.

At sixty years old and two years as head of the CIA, the director's face was lined and craggy. Balding and of average height George Stanford was still an imposing figure dressed in a black suit, white shirt with a black silk tie, and a buttoned up charcoal gray vest with silver buttons along its front. He was the essential gray-man-in-a-suit figure that fit well in the CIA.

"Actually Hank I didn't come from D.C., I was out at the Jet Propulsion Laboratory in California. After talking to those guys I wanted to stop by Houston and see you before I brief the president on this new planet everyone is excited about."

George said, following Hank's gesture and sitting down in the overstuffed brown leather chair, one of two flanking one another in front of the NASA director's desk.

After declining Hank's offer of a beverage George sat back and steepled his fingers, his wire rimmed glasses reflecting the light from wide open windows behind Hank and then continued.

"I want to get your views on *Barcia's Planet*, or as I am hearing it more and more, it's simply referred to as *Barcia*. I understand this is a Mars sized planet with liquid and frozen water, an expanding oxygen atmosphere, and not only a probable ocean, but it has a large land area. Is that essentially correct?" The director asked and then paused.

Hank too paused a moment. "Well, yes, that's a pretty accurate description of this wandering planet. Analysis is, of course, ongoing. Just today I was apprised of a new discovery. You may have heard of what is called the 'Genesis Rock'?"

Hank asked, and then continued when George nodded.

"It's an igneous rock, produced during volcanic activity, and its actual geological name is anorthosite. This mineral was formed about four billion years ago and was only found, until it was discovered on *Barcia*, in two places in the Solar System, on Earth, and on our moon. The importance of finding it on *Barcia* suggests that *Barcia* was not only formed at the same time as Earth and the moon, but was formed of the same materials and in the same place."

Hank paused, watching George's face to see if he got it, and he did.

"That means that *Barcia* formed right here along with this planet and the moon." George said.

"So that would suggest that something made *Barcia* leave Earth's vicinity and take up a two and a half million year orbit around the sun. And I've heard you NASA folks think it occurred the same time as the mass extinction that killed the dinosaurs. Have I got that right?" He asked.

"Yes, our theoretical team is working on how the three bodies, Earth, *Barcia*, and the moon may have interacted with one another, and how *Barcia* was ejected into deep space."

Hank said, holding up his hand to forestall any question from George and leaned forward earnestly before he continued.

"I have to say here that the discovery of this mineral on *Barcia* was the work of Dr. Halberd Boyle. Hal was found unconscious holding what he knew was something of vital intelligence to us. He had risked his life to obtain it as he knew his suit was low on air. Instinctively he opened his helmet and breathed the thin atmosphere of *Barcia*." Hank said.

"I know of Dr. Boyle as I do the other astronauts of course. He's obviously a brave and dedicated scientist. How is he, has he suffered any ill effects from breathing the *Barcian* atmosphere?" George asked a look of concern on his face.

"He's in a medically induced coma at present and he is isolated for observation in case he was exposed to any pathogens." Hank replied. "But I assume you didn't come to just talk about the crew, what's on your mind George?" Hank asked.

"I don't mean to downplay the concern we all have for both your crew and their important mission. However, I understand that since its close encounter with Mars, *Barcia* is now on a trajectory that will bring it close to Earth again, sort of like the return of a prodigal moon if you will." George said.

"Huh, while we don't have anything that currently shows *Barcia* may have been a moon of Earth, I kind of like that term." Hank admitted.

George nodded and continued. "I also understand that orbital calculations indicate that this prodigal moon is likely to slip into an orbit in the habitable zone around the sun."

"That's probably a premature assumption, but the data does seem to indicate it may indeed take up a very favorable orbit. There are many factors to consider, its speed upon arrival, how it will react to the sun's gravity, what plane it will actually orbit in and whether it will interact with the Earth for good or ill. What are you driving at George?" Hank asked, although he thought he knew.

"Premature perhaps, but based on the best data we have, and do you think it's possible that *Barcia* will take up a favorable orbit in relation to the Earth and the sun?" George asked outright.

"Yes George, without a doubt its possible and I have to say it looks very favorable. And I understand your interest and of course the interest of the whole world." Hank offered, spreading his hands.

"And that's just it Hank, the whole world is interested. That includes all the space faring nations consisting of us, the EU who have a ship on *Barcia* as well as we do, the Chinese who have a ship that was ready to go to Mars and could easily go to *Barcia* instead, and the Russians. The Russians have let their manned space flight lag but could readily pick it back up." George said, using his hands to emphasize his words.

"I get the point George *Barcia* is a whole new world of untouched resources and may be able to absorb Earth's overflowing population of billions of human beings." Hank said.

"That's exactly it Hank. *Barcia* may be ready for us to colonize; we could move millions of people there, eventually maybe a billion or more. That would make us a two planet species, roughly equivalent to a type I civilization on the Kardashev ranking scale, our chances of survival as a species enhanced double fold. There has never been such an opportunity for mankind since we left Africa!"

George paused a moment for effect and then continued.

"We certainly don't want our traditional enemies, Russia and China to get a foothold on the planet. And although the Europeans are our allies, we need to be able to control what happens on *Barcia*."

He stopped a moment and it was his turn to hold up his hands as Hank started to reply.

"This is a profound matter of our national security. We discovered *Barcia* first, we landed on *Barcia* first and since Maritime Law governs outer space, we have first claim to the planet. A claim we can defend with armed force!"

George said in a strong voice and then continued.

"Yes, the European Union has a ship on *Barcia*, but that ship would not even be there if the *Astraeus* had not assisted them."

"I understand what you are saying George, but even if a third of our four hundred million population were willing to immigrate, say a hundred and thirty million, we would not use more than a fraction of the available resources!" Hank exclaimed.

"That would be damn near perfect!" George said. We can then allow selective immigrants to take up occupations and lives on a U.S. controlled *Barcia*. With a strong space defense force she would never fall under any power hostile to America! We need to lay claim, in the name of the people of the United States, to the entirety of *Barcia*!"

Hank got up from his desk and went to the windows and looked out although he really didn't see the scene before him as his mind was churning. He was both repelled and attracted to George's idea. It would be a validation for the existence of NASA, a true fulfillment of its mission to the nation. Without turning around he said.

"What do you need from me George? How can I further your idea along?" He asked.

"I need your support Hank I am going to propose we claim this planet, us alone, to the president. I want you to come along and support me on this. Think of it Hank, NASA would have an unlimited budget, we will need hundreds of more ships to include really heavy lifters and thousands of new astronauts both civilian and military. More scientists, more civilian administrators, more equipment, more supplies, more of everything on a scale that will make our efforts in WWII or the space race pale in comparison! We will need thousands more of soldiers and space marines because believe you, we will be opposed. The Chinese and Russians will scream to high heaven. The Europeans will object but not so much because we will give them a role to play on the greatest stage ever.

You can bet these ideas are going through the minds of our opponents right now. I want you to come with me without delay to the White House. I don't mean to sound like a television drama, but there is, literally, no time to lose!"

SEPTEMBER 16, 2049
PLANETARY ARRIVAL PLUS 17 DAYS
OVAL OFFICE, WHITE HOUSE, EARTH

Despite the fact his maternal grandfather lived to become balder than a basketball, President William Tiberius Carswell possessed a full head of hair. Admittedly, at fifty-eight years of age it was all silver, but it was also all his own. He was a handsome man, and in the words of at least one well known journalist he was the 'most presidential looking' of the three men who eventually sought the presidency. In a three way race, he had easily outdistanced both main party candidates.

In the second year of his first term, William, who was elected as an Independent, was the first third party candidate ever elected president in the history of the United States. He was just far enough along in his term to begin thinking about becoming the first third party candidate to ever get reelected president. His administration to date was steady, firm, and admittedly, a bit boring. He was starting to realize he needed something to energize and bring excitement to the electorate, something to fuel a new campaign.

William was certainly not blind to the fact that the recent events involving NASA and this new planet just might be the catalyst he was looking for. If *Barcia* actually took up an orbit in the sun's habitable zone, it would have a giant impact on world politics and most especially the United States.

Laying the morning brief on his desk he turned his chair around and looked out the window of the Oval office. Directors Stanford and Russell of the CIA and NASA were requesting to see him as soon as possible today. And that fit right in with what he was thinking about. There was no doubt in his mind but that they wanted to talk to him about *Barcia's Planet.*

His view out the window focused as the White House gardener, ironically named Mrs. Irene Gardener, and her young female intern came into view. Curious, William slightly bent his six foot two inch frame over and rested his hand on the window sill to better see what the two women were doing.

Mrs. Gardener pointed out a somewhat withered rose bloom on a lower bush and the red haired intern bent over to snip it off. The view brought a smile to William's lips.

"Good thing Bill Clinton's not still president". He muttered to himself.

He turned away from the window and reached up to adjust his red silk tie that boasted gold wire threaded stripes that slashed diagonally across its front. He seemed to remember his tailor mentioning it was an Italian made tie. Reaching, he took his dark blue suit coat from the back of his desk chair, a habit the First Lady was always scolding him for, and slipped it on. Just as he settled the coat on his broad shoulders his view screen intercom pinged and he responded "Yes Connie?"

The view screen, activated by the president's voice only, lit up to show pert, pretty, and brunette Connie Smalls smiling at him as she always did. "I wanted to let you know Mr. President that directors Russell and Stanford are here in the waiting room. They said they can wait as long as you need them to sir."

"Okay Connie, is Mycroft around here?" William asked, referring to Mycroft Holmes, his chief of staff. Mycroft's dad, John Holmes, was a big fan of the fictional detective Sherlock Holmes. When his son was born he naturally wanted to name him Sherlock Holmes. However, his wife strenuously objected and told him he could name him anything but Sherlock. So his dad named him after Sherlock's fictional smarter brother, Mycroft.

"No sir, he's holding a meeting with the heads of the departments." Connie replied.

William paused he knew Mycroft wouldn't like him seeing the two directors without him being present. But what the hell, he was the President, not Mycroft.

"Wait about five minutes and show them in Connie, and have some refreshments sent in as well, thanks." William said. He always made it a point to thank his staff for their service to him.

He stepped toward wall to his left, and facing the painting hanging there, he reached and pushed the hidden button. The painting dissolved and revealed a lighted mirror.

Gustav Einmann, the White House decorator, suggested the frame to him. All the paintings displayed were new by both established artists and the up and coming. The paintings changed daily, or when he changed them by using the mirror. Satisfied he looked presidential enough he pushed the button again.

The picture that came up was a very new painting that startled William, and a little bit superstitious, he took as an omen. It was the artist's rendition of

Barcia's Planet looking very Earth like with blue skies, white clouds, and showing oceans, continents, and islands. Behind the planet was Mars depicted in an almost angry aspect with powerful strokes of yellow, red, and ochre smeared across its surface. William really liked it and looked down to note the signature but it was hard to read. He'd have to ask Gustav…

Still looking at it over his shoulder he moved onto the rug with the presidential seal just as the door opened and the two men came in.

Stanford was slightly in the lead and William said "George, good to see you again!" He said as he offered his hand. "And you, Hank, big things are happening in the cosmos, I bet NASA folks are quite busy and happy!" William continued, also shaking Hank's hand and then leading the two of them to the twin couches set across from one another.

They waited until William sat down and then followed suit. "Thank you for taking the time to see us sir." George said.

"When would I not have time to see the chiefs of two of my administration's most important and influential agencies?" William asked rhetorically.

A team of servers came into the room with a cart of coffee, orange juice, breakfast sausage pieces on toothpicks and a variety of sweet rolls and doughnuts. After they had helped themselves to the refreshments William continued.

"So gentlemen, I assume the two of you are here to discuss that." He said, nodding at the painting of *Barcia's Planet*.

"I've never been able to surprise you with anything Mr. President." George said. "Yes, we want to speak to you specifically about the wandering planet. It is our considered opinion that under the auspices of maritime law, the U.S. should lay claim to the entirety of the planet in the name of the people of the United States." He continued.

William sat back and took a moment. "Well George, I think you have managed to surprise me. How and why should we make such a claim? I'm pretty sure the rest of the world might challenge us on that claim."

This time it was Hank who spoke up. "Mr. President we and I mean the United States, initially discovered the planet, and were the first to land upon it. Under the law as I understand it, we have the right of first claim." He said.

"And there can be no doubt Mr. President we are the only nation wealthy enough and strong militarily strong enough to take, colonize and administer an entire planet for the benefit of all mankind." George added.

"I can see that, China would want to carve out a chunk to send some of their teeming millions to, Russia is not strong enough in space craft or military power to do it, and the EU with their fractious union is not politically strong enough. All the other nations who have launch capability have no manned ships to launch." William said.

"*Barcia* needs one government, not a conglomeration of competing states." George added, noting that the president had almost made their argument for them.

"It's going to cost us though and I mean in billions and billions of dollars. Plus we'd have to act quickly to gear up our production of ships, and the training of astronauts both civilian and military. We'd need emergency funding and eventually authorization from congress. But if we can show a return on our investment I don't think we'll have a problem selling this idea." William said and then paused a moment.

"We will need more launch sites in places like Burns Flats in Oklahoma and we should be able to use some Air Force bases for launching, even Area 51. This will mean a gearing up of production and effort we haven't seen since..." He continued, searching for the right words.

"Since perhaps the national mobilization during World War II sir?" George said, finishing the thought for him. "And I will point out there is a political upshot to all of this sir, it will make for a very lively campaign season, and you will be reelected, not only as the president of the United States, but also of an entire planet!" George pointed out.

William let a little surprise show on his face and said "Yes of course, you're right." He said, as if the thought was new to him. "Well, be that as it may gentlemen, I need to get in touch with our United Nations ambassador." William said, as all three men got to their feet.

"Connie, hunt down Mycroft and let him know I want an emergency meeting of the cabinet." The president said as the two directors exchanged glances, turned and left the Oval Office.

When Hank got back to Houston he had intended to go home and get some needed rest, but as he got in a taxi at the airport his phone rang. He looked at the time, it was 3 a.m. and it was Lowell calling him!

"Lowell, I'm on my way home, can't this wait until morning?" Hank asked.

"No sir it can't, in fact you need to come to the office before you go home." Lowell answered.

"Well, hell, this better be a matter of life or death Lowell that's all I have to say." Hank said, a bit of ice and more than a bit of anger in his voice.

"It is." Lowell replied.

"Whose life Lowell?" Hank said, sitting up a little straighter in the car seat.

"This is an open line sir, I can't say on the phone I'll be waiting for you with a fresh pot of coffee." His chief of staff said and the phone went dead.

Hank looked blankly out the window, his mind churning. "Driver, change of plan, please take me to Clear Lake, Johnson Space Center."

"Yes sir!" The driver said enthusiastically. The trip would be a long one with a good fare and the last one he'd have to drive this night.

SEPTEMBER 17, 2049
PLANETARY ARRIVAL PLUS 18 DAYS
JOHNSON SPACE CENTER, EARTH

Hank picked up the steaming mug of hot coffee and inhaled its aroma. Then he tentatively took a sip of the very hot beverage and then took another deeper one despite its heat. He reluctantly sat the white mug, bigger than a regular cup, emblazoned with NASA's emblem on one side and the word 'director' all in capital letters on the other, on the desktop to his right.

His eyes went to the red folder on his desk bearing the words 'director, eyes only' in white capital letters. He glanced up at Lowell and said "Life or death huh?"

"Well, more life than death Hank." Lowell replied, a smile playing around his lips.

Frowning just a bit Hank opened the folder and picked up the first page of the neatly printed report and began to read. Once in awhile he would purse his lips, frown, frown again, and finally he raised his eyebrows in surprise.

"How sure are they of this Lowell? Any chance of a mistake?" He asked.

Lowell shook his head. "They've done the experiments twice; exobiology has looked at it and they say it's legit. There is no doubt that life; at least on the microscopic level, exists on *Barcia*. And its life that can likely nurture plants, Earth plants." He said.

Hank leaned back, rocking up in his desk chair and sighed. "We better call Director Stanford; we'll let him brief the president on this one." He said, reaching for his mug of coffee which had grown cold.

"And if I'm gonna stay here for the rest of the day, I need a refill on this."

SEPTEMBER 19, 2049
PLANETARY ARRIVAL PLUS 20 DAYS
BARCIA'S PLANET

John, assisted by Jacque D'Artan used the built-in lever system to raise the heavy air lock door into place at the entrance to what the crew dubbed 'the hab', short for habitation module. The one third less gravity on *Barcia* gave them an assist which helped alleviate the almost hourly arrival of rain showers. Despite the manual labor they still managed to swap aviation stories, and like John's dad always said "The first liar doesn't stand a chance."

Jacque was nearly as tall as John, but of a slighter build. His dark hair and eyes spoke of a Spanish or Celtic heritage. Not only did Jacque have a mustache as John had suspected, but also sported a close kempt beard that followed his jaw line, covered his chin, and ended in a swooping arc at his bottom lip. John envied it, Air Force regulations did not allow facial hair other than a mustache even for airmen assigned to a position millions of miles away.

The first thing John did upon meeting Jacque personally was to praise him for his cool handling of the *Beagle* during the overtaking of, and landing upon, *Barcia's Planet.* Then he joined the Frenchman in a wine salute to one another.

"So John, how then is Hal doing?" Jacque asked as they worked.

"The medically induced coma is slowly loosening its grip, and Trish says he may come around as early as tomorrow barring any complications. The sleep and high oxygen treatment gives his brain time to recover from the effects of breathing too thin air." John replied.

"Aw, this is good, no?" Jacque asked rhetorically as he gripped the pneumatic wrench and tightened the bolts on the air lock door.

John took the moment to pause and survey his surroundings. With each passing day the ice seemed to recede, exposing more of the dark and tan soils that made up the planet's surface. His gaze went to the smoke columns that rose unceasingly from the glacier canyons of the mountains. Everyone was eager to go there and discover what they were, but work on the hab and other buildings was the priority for now. The mists kept rising and enriching the thickening atmosphere with oxygen, hydrogen and other trace gases. Doc said he thought the atmosphere was very much like Earth's millions of years ago.

127

Readings indicated that air pressure was continuing to rise and John realized that all the changes taking place were making the planet more and more suitable to humans. Added to the fact that *Barcia* was barreling toward a rendezvous with Sol in the habitable zone, and it all was a truly amazing event. The odds of it happening had to be millions to one, and yet it was happening! It was as though the hand of Providence was bringing a precious gift to humanity, a new and quite livable planetary home.

As remarkable as it was it was not the first time this event happened. All the elements were present for life to evolve on Earth, life that eventually led to the evolution of humankind.

It all started with a benevolent star and a disc of gas that coalesced into a planet in just the right position in its orbit, not to close and not too far from the life giving energy of Sol. And at the same time the planet that became Earth formed a moon that also took shape and became the planet's shield from bombardment of objects from the forming Kuiper Belt. That mysterious region of space filled with millions of celestial objects near and beyond the orbit of Pluto.

It was a shield but it was more than that. It became a stabilizing force that controlled the amount of Earth's movement on its axis and brought about the four seasons with regularity.

Without the influence of the moon Earth would swing wildly around on its axis and may not have ever stabilized enough for the development of anything but the most rudimentary forms of life. That the Earth's creation was with just the right amount of all these factors was nothing short of miraculous, a once in a star system's life event.

And yet it was happening again, not in the same manner, but in the same improbable lining up of events that even now was creating another Life Planet. Another home for the one-planet bound humans, a beacon for showing the way to double the chance of survival of the species. And John was getting to witness it!

With the hab completed serious experiments to establish the biological perimeters of the planet could begin. Exploration of the land and even the oceans could be pushed to the fore now that the matter of the team's survival looked more secure.

Their emergency landing on *Barcia* created some problems, not the least of which was the contamination of this unique world with microbes from both Earth and Mars that the team unavoidably brought with them.

To help in locating themselves and making maps Rolf established a GPS system of sorts using the three Marathon probes circling high above in a geosynchronous orbit around the planet. He would tie that system into their communications net and use it in exploring the surface of *Barcia*.

With the habitat ready to occupy Marjorie turned to planting a garden of cool weather vegetables as an experiment, but with real hopes that it would succeed.

There remained members of the ESA crew John had not met other than to acknowledge them briefly in passing. He knew D'Artan and Lady Jane but Dr. St. John and the other four women astronauts were still merely faces in helmets to him.

Nearly a week quickly passed by since *Astraeus* landed on *Barcia*, and when not working on the hab the crew was busy with other tasks.

Informed by NASA that at least three and possibly as many as six resupply ships were already positioned on launching pads, Doc was selecting additional locations deemed suitable for base camps.

That evening both crews, now united in the hab except for Hal who remained in treatment and Trish who was treating him, gathered for a small celebration meal. John smiled when he thought this meal might go down in history as the first thanksgiving on the new planet and not only be celebrated in the future, but a source of many legends similar to those about America's first Thanksgiving. A meaningful glance at his watch display indicated the date was September 19, 2049.

Most of the crew moved into the hab immediately while others maintained their sleeping areas aboard ship as there was no deadline for moving. But John, eager to meet the rest of the crew and to experience the added freedom of extra living space, was one of the earliest to move inside the hab.

Picking up the handset to the landline they had connected to the ships from the hab, John contacted Trish. When she answered he said "Can I bring you anything Trish, they've got some tasty snacks over here." He said.

"No thanks John I'm good, I've eaten and made a little soup up for Hal too." She replied.

"Aw jeez Trish, Hal's come around! That's great news and a reflection of your excellent care. Is he…" He started to ask, trailing off.

"Hal's fine, a little weak from hunger but his mind is as clear as ever. In fact he working a paper he calls 'The Theory of *Barcia's Planet*'. He's sure that he has its origins figured out. He wants to run it by the team when he gets it finished." Trish said.

"That sounds interesting, ask him if he wants me to give the others any message?" John replied. He could hear her talking in the background to Hal.

"He said to tell them he's happy to be back, but right now he has to get back to his writing."

John laughed. "Okay, I'll leave him alone...and Trish...you did a wonderful job!"

John made a point of seeking out and getting acquainted with Dr. Nigel St. John. Nigel was a man of medium height and weight with a somewhat unruly shock of red hair shot through with grey and white strands showing his mature age. Unusual in this day of easily obtained treatment for the correction of eyesight, Nigel sported a pair of glasses. John thought that somehow, they were appropriate for him.

"Dr. St. John, I can't tell you how impressed I am with Captain D'Artan and his piloting skills. He really came through when needed during the approach and landing on *Barcia*." John said.

"Thank you Colonel, he did his job well and quite likely saved the lives of the entire crew. Jacque is a likeable fellow isn't he?" Nigel asked rhetorically and then continued.

"But I must say that you played no small part in our successful landing as well John, if I may call you John. And in return, perhaps you will call me Nigel, we're going to be in close quarters and I see no reason for formality." He said.

John nodded and said "Very well Nigel. Perhaps you could introduce me to the other members of your crew I have not yet met except in brief passing."

St. John smiled, because the other four 'crewmen' John referred to were all women. "I'd be delighted to John." He said.

John followed him toward the folding table near the center of the common living area. They first approached a pretty, slender woman with straight black hair, dark almond shaped eyes, and a dusky hued complexion.

When he and St. John approached she turned toward them holding a drink and when she smiled John caught a glimpse of perfect white teeth between full lips only lightly colored red. She had a small aquiline shaped nose with a dainty upward sloping tip. John estimated her age at a little short of thirty years old.

"Carla, please let me introduce Colonel John Cummings of the *Astraeus*. We have John to thank as well as Jacque for getting us down safely on the planet. John, this is Dr. Carla Suita chief astronomer and our planetary science officer." St. John said.

Carla extended her hand, not in a hand shake but in a more gentile greeting.

"It is my distinct pleasure to meet you Colonel." She said in a deep voice as John took her hand in his and bowed slightly over it in the European fashion.

He found himself replying in the same manner.

"The pleasure is all mine Carla, I assure you." John said, dropping the use of her title.

"And please feel free to call me John, if you will." He continued.

She invited him to join her for a drink, they made small talk and John found himself greatly interested and reluctantly continued on as St. John gently tugged his arm.

"And this is Mrs. Linda Van Venter, the widow of Dr. Willem Van Venter, and mission specialist for the *Beagle*." St. John said.

Mrs. Van Venter nodded at John reaching and shaking his hand. "I regret the loss of your husband Mrs. Van Venter." He said to the somewhat short and buxom Dutch woman.

Her lips were compressed beneath a well shaped nose as she obviously held back tears, her long dark eyelashes hiding a pair of startlingly blue eyes beneath thin dark eyebrows. She wore no makeup, but her cheeks were quite naturally a blush of red.

"Thank you Colonel. Willem died doing what he loved the most, exploring space and seeking knowledge." She replied, and then averted her gaze to the drink in her hand.

Carla slid her arm around the distraught widow as a tear slid down her cheek. "As our mission specialist Linda is well versed in the using of hand tools, and she is fashioning more permanent markers for our lost comrades." Carla said.

A small smile flittered across her face and Linda nodded. "Willem would want me to make his marker last, so I will." She said.

St. John patted Linda on the hand and continued forward, his hand on John's shoulder.

The last woman astronaut John met was a striking Eurasian from Australia named Maelyn Wabash. John later learned that her first name was Chinese and meant 'beautiful spirit'.

Her hair was auburn rather than black and tended to have a slight curl in its shoulder length tresses. Her eyes were brown with hints of gold near her pupils. She was tall and straight and a smile came easily to her shapely lips.

She took John's hand in a warm and firm grip as Nigel introduced her as Dr. Maelyn Wabash of Tungaroo, Australia.

"I'm very pleased to meet you John, I've heard a good deal about you." She said in a somewhat low and but quite feminine voice.

"You have the advantage then Maelyn, what is your area of expertise on the *Beagle*?" John asked, a little flustered at her dignified attractiveness.

She answered his question but later John couldn't quite remember what she had said, something about astrometrics and she mentioned another field of science. He wanted to remain with her for the rest of the evening, but Nigel gently and firmly pulled him away and John reluctantly said goodbye following him.

"You asked about our casualties John and I thought you'd want to hear it first hand, so I've asked Jacque to fill you in. I'll give Dr. O'Brian a copy of our casualty report to the ESA."

Nigel said, stopping and inviting John to proceed gesturing toward Jacque who stood apart from the others near the airlock. A fourth woman that John hadn't met nodded at his approach and walked away, he had only a glimpse of her.

John and the rest of the NASA crew were still in the dark as to the details regarding the deaths of the three ESA crewmen. The information about them could possibly help the Americans avoid a similar fate. John stepped up to D'Artan and nodded.

The Frenchman did not hesitate and started to tell the tale immediately as if it was something he wanted to confess.

"All three of them Louis, Willem, Juan were sitting in their row of seats on Deck C. I was jinking the ship in an attempt to avoid the fast approaching rubble of Deimos. A large group of meteors swung around Mars and lit up the radar screen like so many approaching missiles, which of course they were.

I succeeded in the maneuver and the array of material passed beneath and to the right of *Beagle*. However during the maneuver I moved the ship into the path of two meteoroids so small they were not detectable on radar. As small as they were they were moving at 40,000 miles per hour and possessed a tremendous amount of stored kinetic energy. With that much force their small size was immaterial, they were capable of great destruction."

Jacque paused a moment and took a sip of his drink, glanced at his shoes, looked up at John, and continued.

"It penetrated the skin of the ship, slightly damaged our propulsion system and left the ship immediately. The second pebble sized meteor penetrated the port side of the space craft and pushed through the hull, pushing its way through the radiation dampening water in the inner shell of the wall and entering Deck C.

Not slowing in the slightest it first struck the arm of Louis D'Angello who was in the act of standing up from his seat. It took his arm off just below the shoulder, and then continued on through the chest cavities of both Willem and Juan who were still seated. The impact was like an explosion inside their bodies with resulting massive tissue expulsion all over the interior of that section of deck. The meteoroid then exited the starboard bulkhead in the same manner it had entered the ship.

The chemical plugging mechanism for sealing the two ruptured bulkheads was both successful and instantaneous. Any loss of atmosphere or water into space was negligible.

Louis' self sealing space suit also worked perfectly and clamped off the arm of the suit immediately, providing a tourniquet and stopping the bleeding. Because of that, Louis survived the initial traumatic amputation of his right arm. But the shock not only of his own injury but also the virtual obliteration of his two crewmates from the waist up, combined with the delay of us reaching him proved too much. He died shortly after we got to him."

"Why was there a delay getting to him Jacque, did your hull penetration alarm not sound?" John asked.

"It did indeed sound John, but it took us some moments to reach Deck C, and the carnage was…was quite daunting. Even though Louis was screaming uncontrollably we could not…" Jacque paused, visible swallowing and then continued. "I should say they could not, because I was piloting the ship, they could not initially locate Louis for all the… the, organic debris. He expired just as they got to him." Jacque said, visibly shaken at recalling the event.

"Heroic measures were taken right there to revive him, but to no avail. Thank God Linda was the last to arrive at the Deck C area and they managed to keep her out, obstructing her view of Willem, or what was left of Willem.

The amount of blood inside three humans is phenomenal, especially in the weightlessness of zero-gee as it spread everywhere. It was a horror show John.

Images of the event reached Earth and by now a significant percentage of Earth's population has viewed them in detail. There is talk of calling our ships home and stopping all ESA human exploration of space."

John could just stand and stare at Jacque, slowly taking in the enormity of his words. "My God!" He said, and then turned away.

There was yet one more female astronaut for John to meet, the same woman who had walked away as he approached Jacque, but he was too distracted by the vivid description of the event for any more socializing. With a solemn squeeze of the Frenchman's shoulder he stalked away, somewhat oblivious to his surroundings and started to enter the men's quarters.

"Excuse me Colonel Cummings." Came a voice from behind him and John turned around. "My name is Isadora Fontana." The woman said, extending her hand in greeting.

John was taken aback; Isadora was, by anyone's criteria, absolutely beautiful. He stuck out his hand and feeling awkward said. "John…please call me John uh…Isadora." He stammered.

The woman smiled and John thought he heard angels sing. She was a complete turnaround from

John's stereotypical view of Italian women. Her hair was blonde not dark, her eyes were blue, not brown, and her complexion was cream, not tanned. The red coveralls worn by the ESA team tried but failed to hide her figure. The white name tag on the left side of her top read 'Dr. Fontana'.

"Ah, Dr. Fontana, may I ask your specialty?" John asked.

"I am the expedition's biologist. *Barcia's Planet* has kept me busy investigating it. But please come, I brought you a juice drink, it sits alongside mine at that table." She said, nodding.

"Yes, of course, thank you." John said inviting her to proceed with a wave of his hand.

"So tell me Dr. Fontana, have your investigations of *Barcia* turned up anything of interest?" John asked as they sat down at the small table.

"It has indeed, and please John, call me Isadora, or Dora as some prefer." She replied.

"But I am sure your biology people have found interesting things too, perhaps?" She said, managing to turn a statement into a question.

John stalled, taking a sip of juice and then said with a wave of his hand. "Oh, I'm sure they have, but I'm a military man, a spaceship driver, my knowledge of such things is rudimentary at best."

"Ah, well, but I'm sure you would know if your scientists have discovered…life on *Barcia*? Because I certainly have." She said, resting her chin in the palm of her hand, her elbow on the table.

"Well, I'm not too surprised Isadora, *Barcia* is very Earthlike. Have you told Dr. St. John about your discovery yet?" He asked, as though just making conversation.

"No, but he has told me something that makes me want to keep your people's secret to myself. It seems your country is about to lay claim to sovereignty over this planet. I think an announcement of life here would complicate that don't you? It could be a rallying cry for those who oppose your claim. And we much prefer you, to the Chinese or Russians." She said.

Instead of replying John lifted his glass and they toasted one another. And then they toasted the EU and the US.

SEPTEMBER 22, 2049
PLANETARY ARRIVAL PLUS 22 DAYS
AREA 51, EARTH

Astronaut and Navy commander Phillip Thomas (Tom) Tucker eyed the massive ship sitting on rails in Hanger 1 at the secret military base known to the world as Area 51. Just a few yards further down the track and deeper into the hanger stood his ship's twin sister which was kind of ironic because his own twin brother, Harold Wayne Tucker, was assigned to that ship.

The rails led out of the hangar door and south to a set of twin launch pads. Phillip's ship named the *USS Trathen* and the second ship the *USS Black* were both the militarized version of Lockheed Martin's heavy lift spaceship, the same ship built for NASA. Both were commissioned U.S. Navy ships and both carried a complement of Army rangers. They were, bluntly put, U.S. warships. And although the *Black* was commanded by an Air Force officer, the ship 'belonged' to the U.S. Navy.

In the tradition of the Navy, the name of the first ship built in a new class of ship gives its name to the entire class. So both the *Trathen* and the *Black* were *Trathen* class ships. With an eye to the future of the

Navy in space and in expectation of bigger future ships, these first two were designated space destroyers. So the official designations of the two ships were the *USS Trathen SDD 100*, and *USS Black SDD-101*. Together, the two ships formed the first military squadron of U.S. space faring vessels and were dubbed the *Black Cat Squadron* after the original destroyer squadron of that name.

Both ships were scheduled to launch in one week's time, so both would start their slow journey to the launch pads today.

Even though he was expecting it, the blaring of the klaxon indicating that the *Trathen* was about to move startled Tom. Huge electric motors cycled up and with just the slightest jolt, the giant wheels of the car carrying the ship began to rotate. At almost the same moment the doors to the hanger began to slide slowly open. The *Trathen* would roll for two hours before the klaxon announcing the start of the *Black's* journey would sound. This would give plenty of room between the two vessels in case there was some kind of problem during the transit.

Dividing up the mission among the different services the soldier complement of the ship consisted of Army rangers rather than marines. There was a half squad, or five men under the command of a grizzled master sergeant who made up one of the five. The other squad members consisted of a platoon sergeant, a staff sergeant, a sergeant, and a corporal. Harold Tucker was the staff sergeant among the second half squad aboard the *Black*.

Tom and his counterpart on the second ship Air Force lieutenant colonel Lucas Flowers were the only members of the two ships crew on hand. The rest of the crew, minus the rangers, was on leave. The rangers were somewhere out in the desert going through their final training cycle. There was no break for those guys.

Warship pilots were recruited from all branches of the armed forces, the Coast Guard, and civilian test pilots. All pilots were openly trained as astronauts by NASA but the ships were secretly constructed on the Groom Lake base itself. All parts were shipped in to the base clandestinely and assembled inside hangers. They were conceived as warships long before the discovery of *Barcia* but intended for just such an eventuality. U.S. national authority believed they were the first and only space-faring warships in the world.

Each warship was armed with chemical laser cannons, kinetic projectile launchers, rocket powered missiles, and the most powerful of all, tactical nuclear weapons.

The rangers, the ship commander's ground troops, were extensively trained beginning with basic combat training and advanced infantry training. These introductory courses were then augmented with parachute training at the Army jump school where each soldier became a qualified paratrooper. This was followed by the grueling many weeks of the "toughest combat training course in the world", the Army ranger school.

After this standard and specialized training, two ten man ranger squads were selected to go on to Space Weapons and Tactics School located on Area 51 itself. Besides learning how to fire and maneuver in zero-gee, they learned how to assault, board and neutralize a spaceship that attempted to resist. Ten of the men would deploy with the two initial ships and ten remain Earth-side as backup. Since the discovery of *Barcia* more warships were under construction and more rangers were undergoing training.

Now, the first deployment of the two fully armed and manned warships, in complete violation of nearly all international space treaties, was imminent. The ships would launch the same time the three resupply ships launched, further concealing their warship identities.

Tom was satisfied with the progress of the *Trathen* as it inexorably traveled down the rail, now approaching the open hanger doors. Then, someone called to him and Lucas, beckoning them to the hanger's office area. They stepped inside just as someone finished running the television screen back and started it forward.

An anchorman was sitting at his news desk while a screen behind him showed a picture of a launch pad. Tom could see the ship was Chinese by its markings even if the small Chinese national symbol wasn't displayed in the top left corner of the scene. The anchorman was speaking.

"The Chinese announced today the resumption of their manned mission to Mars with this launch of the *Lùhng*, Chinese for Dragon. The *Dragon* lifted off just an hour ago from the main Chinese launch site in Manchuria. A government spokesman stated that with the departure of both the American and European space teams from the Red Planet, it was incumbent that China continues with its mission.

The *Dragon* is under the command of Colonel Li Chao Cheng of the People's Army. Colonel Li is their most experienced astronaut; he has commanded several of their space missions."

What neither the reporter nor his audience knew was that a last minute substitution in the crew was made, with a diplomatic officer added to the roster. This officer was authorized to lay claim to any area or site upon which the *Dragon* landed in the name of the Peoples Republic of China

Quietly all the rest of the crew was replaced with military astronauts. The night before in the wee hours of the morning, all scientific gear was removed from the ship and replaced with an assortment of ground weapons. But the ship itself had no weapons other than laser cannons similar to those of U.S. resupply ships.

In the background video, the tail of the *Dragon* lit up with fire from its engines while steam from the water cooling system rose in white clouds and the spaceship lifted off. According to the time stamp in the bottom right corner of the screen, the Chinese had lifted off nearly an hour ago.

Tom and Lucas hurried back outside just in time to hear the electric engine of the sleds where the two warships sat, cycle up to twice the speed. The rollout time was now cut in half. A phone call to the rangers' space training site suddenly ended their training.

An officer picked up a phone in the hanger office and the first call was made to the ship's crew, terminating all leaves.

The value of the soon to arrive *Barcia's Planet* was apparent to the Russians as much as anyone else. Caught with the pants of their spacesuits down, they were scrambling to evaluate their remaining manned space craft. Despite their curtailment of human space exploration for the present, they still had a variety of capsule type spaceships they could place atop their powerful rockets.

While it was true they had little capacity for deep space exploration, it was also true that *Barcia's Planet* would soon not be in deep space. Their own orbital plots showed that NASA and ESA were right; the wandering planet was on a nearly direct glide to taking up an orbit in the habitable zone. Exactly where that would be was still unclear, but it was coming. Anticipating a call from the Kremlin sooner rather than later they were busy getting the answers to the inevitable questions.

In the space program director's office, the red phone connected to the Kremlin began to ring.

SEPTEMBER 25, 2049
PLANETARY ARRIVAL PLUS 26 DAYS
AREA 51, EARTH

For liftoff every crew member of the *Trathen* had their spacesuits on from Commander Tom Tucker down to Corporal Seth White, the lowest ranking Army ranger aboard. Both Tom and his co-pilot Major McEdward Lawson, USAF were on their backs looking up and scanning the complex instrument panel in front of them. Most of the lights were already green but a few were still glowing yellow, indicating the systems they monitored were not yet ready for launch.

Tom was monitoring the background chatter of launch control, but saying little himself. His hands moved across the panel toggling switches and adjusting levels. Finally, all the lights were green and Tom nodded in satisfaction.

"Launch control *Trathen* shows green across the board, standing by."

"Roger *Trathen* acknowledge you are standing by." The control officer replied. "Prepare for final countdown."

"All ranges are clear; all air corridors are clear, standby for immediate launch. Thirty seconds and counting. The countdown continued until FIVE...FOUR...THREE...TWO...ONE..."

A flame flared beneath *Trathen's* base and quickly grew in intensity, spreading out into flaming flower petals as it struck the hardened concrete pad. It was instantly doused by the cool water system and steam rose in a billowing white cloud. The few spectators more than a mile away suddenly felt the concussion of ignition and the roar of the engines engulfed them in a physical impact of sound.

The ship seemed to pause and then lifted upward for its first flight.

"WE HAVE LIFTOFF! GOD SPEED YOU MEN OF THE TRATHEN!"

The screaming roar of the engines at full throttle surged over those watching and rattled the hangers two miles away. It became one huge wave of sound that continued to wash over the launching pad area as the ship lifted faster and faster into the air. Destined to spend its life in space, it would never traverse the blue skies of Earth again.

The engines continued to throttle up and their fading throaty roar became more guttural as the *Trathen* reached the upper vaults of the atmosphere and then pierced the black bubble of space. The engines continued to fire, now silent in the folds of dark space. Finally, the rocket engines flamed out and *Trathen* continued at thousands of miles an hour. Inside, the crew experienced weightlessness, some of them for the very first time except in training. From down in the bottom of the ship came a cheer in unison from the rangers "Hooah!"

In the command center on the top deck Tom and Mac looked at one another and grinned.

Quickly attaining orbit the *Trathen* would whip around in Earth orbit only twice to obtain the gravitational boost the home planet provided before breaking orbit and vectoring toward *Barcia's Planet*. By the time they were halfway around their first orbit the *Black* had launched in their wake. The two warships were soon followed by the launch of two resupply ships from Edwards Air Force Base in California and a third ship from Cape Canaveral.

By speeding up their procedures despite the objections of safety engineers, the five U.S. ships launched only a day plus six hours behind the Chinese vessel *Dragon*. The two warships, their engines bigger and faster than the supply ships, were now in hot pursuit of the Chinese ship. With their beefed up rockets they fully expected to catch the *Dragon* before it reached *Barcia's Planet*.

Luna Base radar indicated that the prodigal planet was the direction the Chinese were headed, not toward Mars. But it also detected that the engines of the *Dragon* were fully as powerful as those of the two destroyers. If the Chinese made it to *Barcia* they would likely have to confront them on the ground.

"Master Sergeant Thompson do you read?" Tom said into his helmet radio.

"Thompson here sir, I read you five by five." The leader of the rangers said.

"Your men can remove their helmets now. The Chinese ship has a good head start on us and I don't see *Trathen* catching them before planet-fall. You may want to prepare your guys for a ground operation." Tom said.

"Yes sir, will do uh, skipper." The ranger said, dipping into the unfamiliar Navy vernacular.

"Thanks chief." Tom replied, addressing the master sergeant as he would a Navy master chief. They were going to get along fine.

SEPTEMBER 28, 2049
PLANETARY ARRIVAL PLUS 29 DAYS
WHITE HOUSE, EARTH

Two well known TV anchormen, Jason Pagano and Mike Harkin of *World Wide News*, better known as WWN, appeared on the TV screens of millions of people worldwide. A voiceover in a deep and mellow tone said "This is a special presentation of World Wide News."

"Good evening." Pagano opened, looking straight into the camera, his pleasant but slightly pudgy face handsome in its own way.

"President William Carswell called for this special address to the people of the United States and the world, calling it 'A matter of international importance'. Although we don't know the actual reason for this announcement, there is speculation it has something to do with the international team of astronauts on *Barcia's Planet*. Here now is our science expert and former NASA astronaut, Mike Harkin, with a recap of what we do know, Mike."

Harkin was a handsome forty-something with dark well trimmed hair and a very dapper blue suit and white shirt sporting a matching blue tie embellished with silver stars. Clean shaven and with slightly cleft chin he was known for his upbeat reporting style.

"Thank you Jason. Well, we do know that the six American and seven European astronauts are doing very well on *Barcia*. That is the inevitable nickname for the world that has come down in the history of space as *Barcia's Planet*. As everyone knows the 'new' planet was discovered a little over three months ago by Dr. Trish Barcia of the Mars Observation Team.

Reports indicate the planet is growing increasingly habitable for humans each day. Despite this very positive turn of events there remain skeptics who see the planet as a physical threat to Earth as it takes its place in the Solar System, or as a possible trap sent by hostile aliens to ensnare unsuspecting humanity. NASA scientists as well as scientists from around the world however, assure us this is a very fortunate, but quite natural event unfolding before our eyes on a cosmic level."

"So you think President Carswell is going to expound on the great benefits that *Barcia* is bringing to all of humanity?"

"That's certainly a possibility Jason, but scientists are doing a very good job of that and the world at large is very excited about all of this. However, I think it also possible that the president may have more than that on his mind."

"Well, we'll leave it at that Mike I understand the president is now ready to speak." Pagano said.

The television cut away to the interior of the Oval Office and the image of President Carswell. He was seated behind the *HMS Resolute* desk, named for the British arctic explorer ship *Resolute* that provided the wood for its construction. The desk was presented to President Rutherford B. Hayes in 1880 by Queen Victoria and was now officially referred to as the Oval Office Desk. The presidential seal was added later by President Ronald Reagan.

Behind the president was the sun dappled windows of the office framed by the presidential and U.S. flags.

A voiceover said: "Ladies and gentlemen, the President of the United States."

"My fellow Americans, I want to start by saying I think that this day will become a day of national remembrance. As you know, on this past August thirty-first, the brave astronauts aboard our spaceship *Astraeus*, landed upon *Barcia's Planet*. They were later followed by the men and women of the European Union's vessel *Beagle*.

The crew of the *Beagle* suffered casualties during the trip to the planet and to their families I want to express the sincere regret of the people of the United States for their loss. However, despite this setback both teams have worked hand in hand to establish the first settlement of mankind on *Barcia*.

As a result of these momentous events, and in consultation and with the agreement of our European allies, the United States, acting in the best interest of the people of Earth, hereby lays claim of sovereignty over *Barcia's Planet* in its entirety.

Some will want to know why we have taken this unprecedented action. To them I say there comes a time when, in the course of human events, the bold must step forward and do what must be done to further the future of our common humanity. World War II was such a time and America stepped forward. That time has come again, that step must be taken again, and the United States of America is the best nation on this Earth to take just such a bold step.

Some will question our right to do this and to them I say history is on our side. It was our Martian Observation Team that made the initial discovery, it was our spaceship that made the initial landing, and it was our astronauts, alongside those of Europe, that laid the stones of the first settlement. I want to make it clear that our claim of sovereignty is unequivocal and if pressed, we will defend it in a court of law or, if necessary, by the force of arms.

In the following days additional U.S. spaceships will launch for a rendezvous with our people on the U.S. Federal Territory of *Barcia's Planet* for the dual purpose of resupplying the settlers there and defending the territory from any encroachment.

Inside the hour our ambassador to the United Nations, Dr. James Shields, will lay our claim of sovereignty before that world body.

I want to assure the world that the Territory of Barcia's Planet will not be an American monopoly. However, as a federal territory U.S. law will prevail there. Orderly immigration from the U.S., the EU and every other nation will be encouraged and accepted under our laws of immigration. The peoples of the nations of the EU in recognition of their moral and material support of our territory will enjoy most favored national union status for immigration to our territory.

Thank you, God bless America, and God bless the United States Territory of Barcia's Planet. Good night."

As soon as the light went out on the camera William turned toward his chief of staff. "Mycroft, get your people working on the key members of congress, I want this declaration ratified ASAP! If we falter, if we blink the world will be on us in a flash and we could lose this opportunity." He said.

"All ready on it chief, I had people with the key figures while they watched your announcement. Many, even most have already agreed to support this move." Mycroft replied with a smile.

"Many, most... by God I want everybody on board this thing! Make sure they know if they don't get on this wagon train to the stars their asses will be replaced in the next election in less than two years! You're my mad dog Mycroft I want you to sic 'em!" The president said with emphasis.

"Damn, there for a minute I thought you were a reincarnation of Theodore Roosevelt. We'll sic 'em sir!"

SEPTEMBER 28, 2049
PLANETARY ARRIVAL PLUS 29 DAYS
WORLD WIDE NEWS, EARTH

The TV screen once more showed the faces of the two WWK anchormen in their New York studios. Behind them a large view screen showed the hall of the general assembly. There was some milling around of members carrying papers and consulting with one another.

"Wow Mike, I admit that caught me by surprise." Pagano said.

"I think it's fair to say Jason that it's caught everyone, and by everyone I mean the world, by surprise. This is without saying, going to be controversial." Harkin answered.

Putting his hand up to the speaker bud in his ear Pagano said. "Not surprisingly I'm getting reports from around the capitals of the world that there is jubilation, confusion, outrage, acceptance and rejection of President Carswell's words. This has really stirred up the proverbial hornet's nest.

They're telling me we are cutting away to the United Nations where Secretary General Jack Straw of Australia is attempting to gavel the representatives into some semblance of order." He said.

"Order, order, we can't debate the subject of *Barcia's Planet* until we come to order." Straw said, continuing to pound his gavel on the podium. As a sullen hush fell, he looked at Ambassador James Shields and said.

"Ambassador Shields, does the United States have an issue to bring before this body?" He asked.

As the U.S. ambassador got to his feet the hall was deathly quiet, an air of breathless expectation was almost palpable. "Yes, Mr. Secretary, we do." He answered.

Secretary General Straw looked around the room as it continued to be silent. "You have the floor Ambassador Shields, what is it?" He asked.

"Mr. Secretary General, members of the United Nations General Assembly, regarding the planet known as *Barcia's Planet*... the United States of American hereby lays a claim of exclusive sovereignty." He said, and then sat down.

The assembly erupted in a maelstrom of objection, confusion, acceptance, rejection and everything in between. Once more, after gaveling the hall to silence Jack Straw said.

"I understand that the Russian ambassador and the ambassador of China have a joint statement that they want the ambassador of Canada to read.

Ambassador Mathews, are you willing to read this statement?" The Secretary General asked with a puzzled look on his face.

The camera cut to a close up of Ambassador Joseph Mathews, an up and coming politician from Ontario. He was a good looking man, young with light brown hair, clean shaven and with a wholesome look. He was tall and slim and well dressed in a light gray suit, vest, light blue shirt and a white tie with small red maple leaves running diagonal along its length.

"I know this is unorthodox Mr. Secretary General, but I felt obliged to acquiesce to their request, if I may?" He asked.

Straw waved his gavel dismissively and said. "Yes, yes, please get on with it sir."

Mathews frowned slightly and said. "We, the space faring nations of Russia and China will never recognize this false and brazen American claim. The fruits of space are open jointly to all the nations of Earth and we find the stand of the United States unacceptable at any level. It will be resisted to the utmost ability of our nations and we call on the other space faring nations of India, Pakistan, North Korea and Vietnam to stand with us as they have in the past, in resisting this American imperialist land grab."

As Mathews finished speaking the delegations of China and Russia walked out, and the cameras followed them.

Inside twelve hours their embassies filed letters of protest against the American claim, protesting in the most vociferous diplomatic language.

SEPTEMBER 28, 2049
PLANETARY ARRIVAL PLUS 29 DAYS
ALPHA BASE, BARCIA'S PLANET

With each passing day Hal's strength got better and better. He almost felt ready to restart his geological survey of the surface again, although in his absence Marjorie had filled in. And done a good job he admitted. But he had used his time well and yesterday gave a copy of his completed thesis on *Barcia* to each of them. He asked them to read it over and be prepared to discuss it this afternoon when most routine chores were over.

Doc was especially glad to see him working again and welcomed the document. "I will give it my undivided attention Hal." He had said.

Hal pulled out his printed copy and for the umpteenth time read it over for any last changes he might want to make.

Writing and reading on the computer was fine, but for the real feeling of completion, Hal always preferred to see his work printed on paper, there was just a finality to it that he did not get when he simply clicked and stored a file in the depths of the machine, regardless how efficient it was. He was always nagged by the thought his work might just disappear. Laying the copy on his small lap desk he took his pencil from behind his ear and used the graphite point to guide his eyes as he read.

The Triple Ring Theory
On the origins of Barcia's Planet
By Dr. Halberd Boyle

One of the more popular of the current theories on the formation of our moon suggests that the Earth and Luna formed at the same time out of the same gaseous materials ejected from the sun.

The theory is that both bodies formed from disks of this gaseous material 4.6 billion years ago. In the past I have supported that theory, and it forms the backbone of the *Triple Ring Theory on the Origin of Barcia's Planet.*

I believe, for reasons I shall expand upon, that when the rings of material that eventually became Earth and Luna took shape, there was a third ring. This ring formed around the Earth and outside the orbit of Luna. Here are the reasons I think this is so.

1) The presence on Barcia's Planet of the mineral *anorthosite* also known as the *Genesis rock.* This mineral formed more than 4.5

billion years ago on both Earth and Luna indicating that both these bodies formed at the same time and from the same materials. By extension then it also, by its presence on the planet, indicates that Barcia's Planet also formed at the same time and from the same materials.

2) In 1959 the first grainy photographs taken by the Soviet spacecraft Luna 3, showed that the far side of the moon lacked any dark areas called maria or seas like those found on the near side. However, it did have plenty of craters showing it was bombarded equally as much as the near side. Why then did it not have volcanic flow from these meteor strikes? The answer became obvious. The far side of the moon is much thicker than the near side. Later, radar scans shows this to be true, the far side is, on average, 30 miles thicker. Theories exist as to why this is so but none of them were really satisfactory until now. The reason the far side is thicker is because of the presence of Barcia's Planet, it's gravitational pull on the moon tugged molten material from the near Earth side of the moon to the far side when Luna was coalescing and becoming a

moon. Barcia's Planet, farther away from Earth and less susceptible to the roiling heat coming off the molten planet, was the first of the three to cool off.

There is only one conclusion to be drawn from this theory. Barcia's Planet began its life as a moon of Earth, a rather big moon, a big moon that was moving away and straining against the pull of Earth. And so it remained for billions of years until only a short time ago, 65 million years ago to be exact. That is when, at the same time it struck Earth and caused a mass extinction, including the demise of the dinosaurs, a large passing asteroid gave Barcia's Planet the gravitational push it needed to escape.

And escape it did, but not just from Earth's pull, but almost from the pull of the sun itself. Failing to escape completely, the Earth's prodigal moon instead follows an eccentric elliptical orbit that takes it away from the inner solar system on a two and a half million year orbit. Earth's Prodigal Moon, Barcia's Planet, has come home, perhaps if our calculations are correct, to stay.

Satisfied, Hal leaned back in satisfaction and smiled. But his relaxation was short lived as into his lab cubicle stepped a very excited Rolf.

"Hal, have you heard the news? The president, in the name of the United States, has claimed sovereignty over *Barcia*! *Barcia's Planet* is now a territory of America!" Rolf exclaimed, and without waiting for an answer went to tell the others.

Hal was somewhat surprised, but this was politics, an area he tried to avoid. They would probably want to talk about that too at the evening meeting. He was a little more surprised when Marjorie popped in.

"Hal, I am so relieved you are recovering so well. I missed you while you were incapacitated." She said.

Hal nodded and smiled. "Thank you Marjorie, it's good to be back. What have you been up too?"

"Well, I wanted you to know that your experiments were a success, we found live microbes in the soil." Marjorie said. "*Barcia* has life!"

Hal smiled again and shook his head. "I don't remember doing any experiments; this is your discovery Marjorie, not mine. Mine is in this folder I'm going to make you guys listen to tonight." He said. "But luckily for you it won't take long. No that discovery is all yours Marjorie and you're welcome to it. Good job!"

That evening they all met in the common area of the habitat with both crews in attendance. With the two crews combined, Hal would make his presentation to twelve people. In an effort of integration the blue coveralls of the NASA team intermingled with the red of those of the ESA.

John found himself sitting in the back row of folding chairs and then, she was there. Isadora stood beside his chair looking down at him. "Is this seat taken?" She asked.

John quickly came to his feet. "No, no of course not." He said. "Please sit down Isadora."

As they both settled in their seats John looked into her beautiful eyes and they smiled at one another. As Doc introduced Hal, Isadora's hand slid into his. They didn't hear much of the lecture. As soon as they could the two slipped away. At the door of the women's dormitory Isabella pulled a dark blue scarf from around her neck and tied it through the ring doorknob.

"What's that?" John asked. But Isadora only smiled and held a finger to her lips and opened the door, pulling him inside.

SEPTEMBER 29, 2049
PLANETARY ARRIVAL PLUS 30 DAYS
ALPHA BASE, BARCIA'S PLANET

"Standby for the President of the United States." The same voice said for about the eighth or ninth time as the crew of U.S. astronauts looked expectantly at the presidential seal on the view screen, placed on a dark blue back ground.

"You suppose this has to do with us declaring *Barcia's Planet* ours?" Rolf said.

"Well, duh!" Marjorie quipped. "If not I'll sure be surprised." She continued.

There was a flicker on the screen and then they working at President Carswell and Secretary of State Elaina Morales.

"Hello *Astraeus*, greetings from the White House. Secretary Morales and I wanted to speak to you today in the aftermath of the United States declaration of sovereignty over *Barcia*. Your European colleagues are receiving a similar brief even as we speak.

As a new territory *Barcia* needs a governor and military commander to execute certain legal tasks that help make our claim even more legitimate than it already is. I've asked Secretary Morales here to outline those tasks for you. Madam Secretary." The president said, glancing at her.

"As the president said the first thing we need is a new governor and a military commander. The governor to take over the administration of the territory and the military commander to insure there is no physical challenge to our claim. To meet these two goals the following appointments are effective as of the date of our sovereignty September 28, 2049."

Dr. Daniel Morgan O'Brian is appointed Governor of the United States Territory of *Barcia's Planet*, to govern at the pleasure of the President of the United States until relieved of such duty.

Lieutenant Colonel John Edward Cummings is, by order of the President of the United States, promoted to the rank of Colonel, USAF and simultaneously appointed military commander of all U.S. Forces upon the planet or in outer space within twenty thousand miles of the planet. To serve as such until properly relieved."

The secretary looked over at the president expectantly who said: "There are certain tasks that need to be accomplished quickly, recorded both in print and on film and sent to NASA. You will receive the template for a U.S. territorial seal that you will replicate on your 3D printer and display on the airlock door to Alpha Base's habitat which is now the operational center for the territorial government. The flag of the United States will be prominently displayed atop or beside the habitat and will be raised in an appropriate manner and the Declaration of Sovereignty document read in public.

All other members of the crew will continue their duties as assigned by Governor O'Brian. That's all for now, a staff member of the State Department will remain online for any questions you might have. I reside special trust and confidence in all of you, thank you and God bless these United States and the Territory of *Barcia's Planet*."

SEPTEMBER 30, 2049
PLANETARY ARRIVAL PLUS 31 DAYS
ALPHA BASE, BARCIA'S PLANET

The crew members were all assembled in front of the habitat, and in response to Doc's invitation so too were the crew of the *Beagle*. If any of the Europeans harbored any resentment at the actions of the United States, they kept them to their selves.

In accordance with instructions the U.S. territorial seal in brass for Barcia's Planet was replicated in the metal forging 3D printer and placed on display on the habitat's airlock. A brass American eagle along with steel pulley for raising the flag was also created. The only thing make from excess building materials was the rolled aluminum tube pole stuck in the ground and rising high enough to properly display a three foot by five foot flag of the stars and stripes.

Isadora stood off to one side with a film camera in her hands. She had volunteered to film the event in response to John's request. Of course everyone was in their spacesuits and helmets and it was hard to recognize anyone. Rolf stood beside the flagpole holding the flag; Trish was also there with her hands on the lanyard, off to their left stood Doc with a tablet in his hands and John standing beside him.

"I want to welcome Dr. St. John of the European Space Agency and the rest of his expedition to this ceremony. We are glad our European friends are present for this auspicious event. In recognition of the formal annexation of *Barcia's Planet* as a territory of the United States, the following citation is presented.

"Greetings from the President and People of the United States of America, now I, William Tiberius Carswell, by the authority vested in me as President by the Constitution of the United States of America, do hereby proclaim *Barcia's Planet* a Territory of the United States from this day forward. In addition I hereby extend the distance of 20,000 miles around this planet to be the territorial space over which the United States exercises sovereignty. In witness whereof, I have hereunto set my hand this 28th day of September, in the year of our lord two thousand and forty-nine, and of the Independence of the United States of American the two hundred and seventy third.

Signed, William Tiberius Carswell, President of the United States."

As the recorded sounds of the 'Star Spangled Banner" wafted over *Barcia* for the first time, Rolf raised the flag with John and Jacque rendering military salutes and the others placed their hands over their hearts. As the flag reached the top and unfurled in the Barcian breeze Doc turned to the assembly and said.

"Please join us in the territorial capital for celebratory refreshments."

The recorded ceremony was sent immediately to NASA for presentation on the evening news.

OCTOBER 31, 2049
PLANETARY ARRIVAL PLUS 62 DAYS
HEADQUARTERS ROSCOSMOS, MOSCOW

Boris Nikolayevich Volkov, the director of ROSCOSMOS or Russpace the Russian Space Agency, looked at the many reports lying upon his desk. Things were progressing well, and these were the latest updates for his inspection. Boris was quite used to all things outer space not just because he was the director of Russpace, but also the son of Anatoly Nikolayevich Volkov, the former director. He did not directly succeed his father for there was another director between the two Volkov men. That director's performance however was less than expected and Boris was promoted into the position just three years later.

Reaching, Boris selected the first report on his left which happened to be the latest update from the two Russian launch sites. Manned space launches were done at the Kazakhstan Cosmodrome, while the more secret military launches were accomplished at the Plesetsk Cosmodrome in northern Russia.

Before he started reading he looked out his office window, noting the early, already heavy snow fall drifting down in cotton ball sized flakes. He sighed, it would be many months before the gray skies of winter were warm and blue again. The streets below were quite busy despite the snow. He looked toward the horizon and could just make out the top of the building housing the space flight operations in the nearby suburb of Korolev.

Boris was glad they were separate from his own facilities; he preferred to be away from operations on a day to day basis where he could think. His family name of Volkov meant 'wolf' and Boris lived up to that name somewhat as a lone wolf. Of course when the situation required it he was not above doing a bit of micromanaging if necessary.

Sitting down he pulled the report in front of him and began to read. Although not fat, Boris worked out four days a week, he was heavy set or what some people might call 'big boned'. He had a thick head of hair that, at age 43, was still coal black. His hair was matched by a thick, black, brush cut mustache that he waxed each morning. Boris liked things black, and so he wore a well cut black business suit.

He found that wearing black tended to emphasize his unusually light grey eyes which did indeed look like the eyes of a Siberian wolf. His only concession to color was the dark red, almost maroon colored tie he wore with a small Russpace pin displayed near the tie knot which some thought looked very much like the design for NASA.

Boris had three powerful 'Moskovi Mark IV' rockets that were quickly modified for the assigned mission to land on *Barcia's Planet*. They would be ready when the new planet came within range of their engines. Two more were under major overhaul and upgrading that he planned to use as his reserve. The Kremlin also ordered that no less than six more Mark IVs be constructed.

To go atop the rockets he had one four man capsule available along with two three man capsules and a second four man due out of construction in a month. That meant that initially Russpace could put three rockets and ten military trained cosmonauts in space by the time they were needed and quickly followed up with a fourth rocket and four more men.

Designed for short near-earth trips to the moon and mining asteroids, the capsules had absolutely no external weapon capability. The crew however was armed with the best hand weapons available. This included not only bullet weapons for planet surface combat, but hand grenades with their own oxygen cylinders, laser rifles and light mortars that were breech loaded with shells that had internal oxygen for ignition. These weapons were stored in the supply rocket along with rations, water and other essentials. The supply rocket would launch from Plesetsk Cosmodrome and rendezvous with the capsules.

The expedition's mission was to carve out a toehold on *Barcia's Planet* lay Russia's claim and hang on for reinforcements while negotiations were carried out for the UN to recognize their claim of sovereignty. It was a desperate mission and the Kremlin knew it.

In the meantime they would brush the dust off their plans for a heavy ship. Thanks to their intelligence the ship was very much like those of the EU. They would not be ready any time soon, but they were no doubt the future. Production plants were already gearing up for manufacture.

The importance of gaining a position on the resource rich planet was a national goal, and not since the Great Patriotic War against the Germans had the Russian state been so electrified. Thousands of new defense sector jobs galvanized the economy, the country was booming!

Boris placed a call to his counterpart in China inquiring about the possible purchase of a ship but was politely and firmly turned away. He then approached India who was about to complete their first five man spaceship modeled after both the American and Chinese design. But they were playing their cards very close to the vest. Intelligence indicated they were waiting to see how the Chinese adventure and the Russian gamble, if there was one, turned out before making any decision. No amount of money or foreign aid could compel them to sell their one ship.

A raid on the Indian space agency by armed force was contemplated but rejected due to the negative repercussions in the United Nations.

However, the Kremlin let him know they were pleased at what was accomplished in such a short time despite the failure to obtain any foreign ships.

To go along with the six additional rockets the national authority authorized a 40 man class of military cosmonauts to undergo training at the space academy in Star City.

A knock at his office door announced the arrival of his assistant Elena who walked in bearing a steaming cup of Columbian coffee made very strong.

Boris nodded at her both in greeting and in farewell as he took the cup with a smile. Elena turned and left without a word.

All in all, Boris Volkov was a happy man. He strolled to the window and looked out once more, taking a drink of the steaming brown liquid as he did so. Perhaps he could expect a step up in his pay grade, soon.

NOVEMBER 17, 2049
PLANETARY ARRIVAL PLUS 79 DAYS
ALPHA BASE, BARCIA'S PLANET

The atmosphere of *Barcia* was continuing to thicken up, air pressure continued to rise and was at 8.5 psi already nearly double the 4.89 psi on the summit of Mount Everest. This level of air pressure was already more than half way to the 14.69 psi at sea level on Earth. If their tests continued to show no pathogens in the air, water and soil of the planet the day would soon come when they could take their helmets off and walk freely in the sunshine. And to date, they had not detected anything dangerous to humans.

"Oh what a day that will be!" Marjorie thought as she walked among the somewhat stunted growth of corn stalks. Of course that was to be expected because it was still very cool, especially at night and the plastic tarp with electric heater was just not warm enough for a good crop yet. She walked around the tarp making sure the pins holding it to the ground were secure. They were, but she stopped in surprise when she found a small hole in the tarp down near the soil. It was a good three by three inch hole and she was puzzled what might have made it.

"Perhaps it was caused by a small meteor strike?" She thought.

She had to bend over after entering the tarp because it was rather short, and she carefully moved among the plants until she could see the hole from the inside.

Unlike the packed dirt outside, she had tilled the soil under the tarp before planting the corn and it was soft and loose. Looking closely at the hole she thought she saw marks in the dirt just inside. She got down on her knees and peered even closer, turning on her helmet's light. Then she caught her breath and the hair on the back of her neck stood up. At the base of three or four cornstalks, about two inches up from the dirt, she found half moon shaped pieces gnawed out. Something had eaten a portion of the stalks!

She quickly backed out of the tarp and pulled her radio off her belt and called Doc. When he answered she said.

"Doc, can you meet me at the corn tarp, something has eaten on some of the plants!" She said.

She got back a "What!?" Soon followed by "We'll be right there!" And before he let the button go on his radio she heard someone in the background say "Aw, jeez!"

"And tell John to go get Isadora, she's gonna want to see this too!" She said excitedly.

It didn't take long for Doc, John, Isadora and then the rest of them not on essential duty to arrive. Isadora produced a camera and with a querulous look at Marjorie who nodded assent, she went under the tarp.

"Go to your right Isadora and about midway down." Marjorie called out. She pulled out a notepad, wrote down the date and time and added the notation 'Found signs macro life on BP'.

Everyone was talking now and asking questions. Someone said "What does this mean?"

"It means that life above the microscopic level never died out on *Barcia*. Some way, somehow it survived the trip through deep space every 2.5 million years for the past 65 million years! It's a bloody miracle!" Marjorie finished almost yelling the last sentence out.

Dr. St. John smiled and said "It is indeed!"

That evening after dinner everyone stayed in the galley area and discussed the new find. The information was sent out to both NASA and ESA but in code. With the growing controversy over

America's claim of *Barcia* things had become a little more cloak and dagger, something the scientists despised.

The upshot of the discussion was that a joint team would set out the next morning to visit the smoke columns. As the warmest spots on the planet all the time, they were the logical place to look for life in perhaps large numbers. They broke up afterward but sleep was late in coming to most of them.

The following morning Doc, John, Isadora and Marjorie readied the rover for the trip to one of the smoke columns they had dubbed 'smokers'. The nearest smoker was the same one Hal had approached before his accident. Doc and Marjorie rode in the front seat with Isadora and John sitting behind them in the bed of the rover. They were lightly equipped with specimen kits and hand digging tools.

The ambient air temperature was well above freezing at 41 degrees Fahrenheit, an early spring day on Earth. The snow and ice continued to recede and precipitation now fell only in the form of rain.

A half hour later they had gone as far as they could in the rover as they reached the foothills. The smoker could be seen further up into the mountains as they dismounted. It was not that far away and after a short rock-strewn walk they approached it. They could now see its entrance was a tunnel with an opening that appeared to rise higher than a standing human. Large boulders kept them from seeing the full extent of the tunnel opening but they could see the dark smoke roiling, gathering in the top of the tunnel to finally exit into the sky.

As they climbed up and over the boulders John was in the lead and the first to reach the boulder top, where he stood up. The others paused and looked up at him when he said "Aw jeez!"

"What is it?" Marjorie said. But John didn't reply, he just stood there as they scrambled up beside him and saw the scene before them.

"Why, it's a meadow full of grass and bushes!" Marjorie exclaimed.

"Hum, looks more like a ground covering succulent and ferns. Both of which are ancient forms of plant life." Isadora offered.

"Yes, and everything seems so moist and growing rapidly in the warm sun." Doc said.

"Get down!" John said, lowering himself just behind the boulder. "I saw something move." He continued. The rest of them followed his example as John toggled his helmet visor to zoom in bringing the scene in closer with the equivalent of 3X power. Once more the others followed his example.

"Look a little to the left of the tunnel entrance." John whispered. "Look just below the largest fern there." He continued.

Isadora caught her breath as she saw what he had seen. There was a small, dark, thickly furred creature sitting just below the plant and as they watched, it reached up and took the bottom limb of the fern in a prehensile hand and drew it to its mouth, nibbling at the leaves.

While pulling the limb down the short-faced animal gave them a profile view of its head. Its hooded eyes were huge and black with eyelids mostly closed against the bright sun. It was obviously adapted to an environment with much less light. It had tall pointed ears that stood high on its head like those of a fox. It sported a bushy tail like a squirrel, about as long as its body. It was a tail that could be curled around the animal's body when the temperature fell.

"It looks like a koala with pointy ears and a bushy tail." Marjorie whispered excitedly.

"Well, I propose we call it 'Cummings Barcian koala' after its discoverer." Isadora said.

"That's as good a name as any for its common name; you'll have to assign it a taxonomical name when we know more about it Isadora." Doc said.

"By the way, is everyone filming this? This is another historical find, the first life found on *Barcia* other than microbes." Doc pointed out.

They all were filming it and stayed for awhile getting images of the creature. Then they were surprised again as John said "I see more of them, smaller and off to the left of the first one."

Sure enough they could see at least four small versions of the animal working their way through the ferns and succulents towards the larger animal. Then they were totally surprised and thrilled when the larger creature lay down and the four smaller ones joined it in what was obviously a suckling behavior.

"Holy cow, they're mammals!" Marjorie exclaimed. "The mother is feeding them milk! How on Earth can that be?" She continued.

"You mean how on *Barcia* could that be?" John offered as Isadora poked him in the side with her elbow.

"It certainly appears that way Marjorie." Isadora said. "This is an even more historical event Doc!" She continued as they all watched in stunned silence.

"Time's getting short folks we're going to have to head back. May I suggest we see if we can get some of the plant material for analysis?" Doc asked.

A few minutes later they were on their way back to the base, with both Isadora and Marjorie clutching precious specimen bags of samples of both the ferns and the succulents.

NOVEMBER 24, 2049
PLANETARY ARRIVAL PLUS 86 DAYS
ALPHA BASE, BARCIA'S PLANET

Trish was on duty in the ship's command center when the call came in.

"Alpha Base, Sparkyfence One, over." Then there was a pause, Trish turned from her work terminal and toggled the radio as the call was repeated.

"Alpha Base, Sparkyfence One, please acknowledge."

"Sparkyfence One, Alpha Base, go ahead" Trish replied.

"Alpha Base, please switch to encrypted channel." The voice said.

Trish only had to push a button to go to the preset channel. The call was not a surprise to her because NASA told them to expect it. It was a call from the commander of the resupply fleet.

"Alpha Base to Sparkyfence One, over." Trish said once the radio had tuned in the frequency.

"Be advised Alpha Base that a bogey, repeat a bogey will arrive your location soonest in approximately two days. Sparkyfence One and Two will follow soon after. Romeo Sierra Three will follow in approximately five days to your exact, say again your exact, location."

"Also be advised Alpha Base that Sparkyfence One and Two are USN ships. Please repeat back, over"

In military jargon Tom Tucker, for that was who was communicating to Trish, told her that the Chinese ship *Dragon* was arriving in two days followed closely thereafter by two U.S. warships designated Sparkyfence One and Two in close pursuit to be followed five days later by three more U.S. resupply ships.

Trish acknowledged and repeated back the full message as she had both recorded and written it down.

"Sparkyfence One, end of message." Was the last she heard from the voice.

Trish took the written message and went to find Doc or John. She found them just preparing to leave the ship and explained she had an important message from the resupply fleet. They all returned to the command center and she read the message out loud to the two of them.

"Sounds to me like it's gonna get real crowded around here." Doc said.

"And hot maybe. He said the first two ships coming in besides the bogey are U.S. Navy, which means they're warships. And the bogey they're chasing has got to be the Chinese ship that was supposedly going to Mars." John said.

"Warships? When did we get warships for outer space?" Doc asked.

"Well, it means we built them in secret, likely at some restricted military or CIA base." John replied.

"You mean someplace like Area 51 John? Trish asked a frown on her face.

"Sure, yeah, that's one possibility." John answered. "The important thing is that it appears the Chinese want to get a ship down on *Barcia* to forestall the U.S. claim to it or at least to get a claim of their own on record. We could find ourselves in the middle of an armed conflict." He continued.

John paused a moment, thinking, and then continued. "If the Chinese land near us and are armed, there would be little we could do to stop them taking the base from us, perhaps even before the warships can get here."

"Do we have any defense John?" Doc asked, spreading his hands in a sign of some dismay.

"We have the *Astraeus* and the *Beagle*, both ships have laser cannons. However, I have my doubts about the *Beagle* since she's been damaged. And of course the EU is not bound to defend our base and our claim to this planet."

"So you are proposing we use the *Astraeus* to do what?" Doc asked.

"We can meet the Chinese ship before it arrives and actually impede their landing; perhaps delay them long enough that the warships will catch up before it gets too serious.

But as for ground defenses we really haven't any. However, we could approach Dr. St. John about removing one or two laser cannons from *Beagle* and mount them on the rover. With a portable generator in the bed a laser bolt hot enough to make things warm for invaders on foot could be generated." John said.

"Okay, I'll get with Dr. St. John and see what can be done." Doc said.

St. John agreed with the removal of at least one laser cannon, so Jacque, assisted by Rolf, began to work on that project. Meanwhile John set out to get *Astraeus* ready for liftoff. The crew unloaded the last of their personal gear and moved it to the habitat.

The following day John finished the system checks on the ship and began the final preparations for departure. As he was finishing up Hal came aboard the ship.

"Hal, I guess you're feeling like your old self." John said.

"I am John and that's why I'm here. I think you need someone to go with you, if nothing else to keep an eye on things while you get a little sleep. I'm completely recovered and want to help."

John looked at his friend and nodded. "I don't have any problem with it Hal; you're welcome to come along. I'll let you approach Doc about it but you can tell him I support your going along." John said.

Later that day Doc and Hal came to see him and Hal was in. The two men finished up their personal business and went to bed early that night. They would launch in the late afternoon the following day.

NOVEMBER 25, 2049
PLANETARY ARRIVAL PLUS 87 DAYS
ALPHA BASE, BARCIA'S PLANET

Jacque and Rolf with help from some of the others managed to transfer one of the *Beagles'* laser cannons to the rover. The rover now looked like a miniature tank with its tracked wheels and the muzzle of the laser jutting from the rover's bed past the back seat and over its hood.

After completing the modification they sat out a short distance in the rover searching for a target. Finding a hostile rock they fired a few red pulses of energy that blew the basketball sized stone into dozens of pieces. There was little doubt but that it was a formidable weapon. Rolf let out a yell of excitement and found a few other targets before the fire demonstration was completed.

Both John and Hal took up station in the command center, and at 1600 hours the *Astraeus* lifted off without a hitch. The engines roared and with thirty percent less gravity than Earth, easily and quickly attained orbit velocity. They planned to orbit around *Barcia* for the rest of the day and then break from the planet's pull to search for the *Dragon* using their far range radars.

Using the prearranged encrypted frequency John attempted to contact the *Trathen*. "*Astraeus* to Sparkyfence Alpha, over". John said and was immediately answered.

"Sparkyfence Alpha, go ahead." Tom replied from his own command center.

"*Astraeus* is circling around *Barcia* and will break orbit in approximately an hour to seek and make contact with your bogey." John replied. "How long before you can join us?" He continued.

"Soonest projected arrival some eighteen hours after you break orbit. We will support your move *Astraeus*." Tom replied.

"Clear. Clear sailing *Trathen*." John replied, as he reached and toggled his radars on.

"You ready for this Hal?" John asked.

"I am Colonel, let's go bogey hunting." Hall said with a grin.

John went through the procedures to prepare the engines for firing, it would about a five minute burn, just enough to break the gravitational hold of *Barcia* and give *Astraeus* a modest forward speed toward the direction of Earth, the direction from where the *Dragon* was coming.

When the burn came, it pushed the two astronauts gently back into their seats for five minutes and then as the main rocket shut off they were back in zero-gee.

Almost immediately the radar picked up the Chinese ship and the two men looked at one another. Then John toggled his radio and said into the clear; "Unknown vessel, be advised you have entered U.S. Barcian Territorial Space, identify yourself."

The two Americans waited expectantly for any peep of a reply, but none came. John used his steering rockets to turn the nose of the ship until they were pointed directly at the *Dragon*.

"Unknown vessel, unknown vessel, you have entered without clearance into Barcian Territorial Space, identify yourself or prepare for interception, over!" John exclaimed, putting a little steel into his voice. Then a reply came to them out of the blackness of space.

"This is the *CPRS Dragon*, of the Chinese People's Republic traveling in open interplanetary space, we do not recognize this planet as a territory of the United States. Please move your ship out of our way; we would not want to have an accident."

NOVEMBER 25, 2049
PLANETARY ARRIVAL PLUS 87 DAYS
BAIKONUR COSMODROME, RUSSIA

Even as John was contacting the Chinese, Director Boris Volkov was behind a reinforced observation bunker where he could see his three rocket ships. Each rocket was on a launch gantry far enough away from the others that an explosion on one would not affect the other two, at least not physically.

He looked through field glasses at the first rocket scheduled to launch, rocket number 3126 that had the four man capsule atop it. Rockets 3127 and 3125 both carried a three man capsule. Volkov was surrounded by engineers, technicians, and military officers. They were gathered because this was a monumental day, the largest launch of Russian spacecraft at one time, ever.

Blue white and red banners festooned the bunker's interior along the walls and around the table in the middle of the room. That table held the bottles of vodka and glasses they would use to toast the success of this new space race. At least everyone hoped they would be drinking toasts.

Volkov lowered the binoculars and looked up at the big screen on the bunker wall. The camera was zoomed in on rocket 3126 and he noted the countdown clock in the lower left corner. As if they knew he was looking the voice of launch control came from the TV's speakers.

"Gotovnosty dyesyat minut…launch in T-minus 10 minutes and counting."

One of the military toadies, a major, stepped toward Boris, his hand extended. "Congratulations Director Volkov, this is a red letter day."

Volkov ignored his proffered hand and replied curtly. "The time for congratulations will come when the last of the rockets have launched safely major."

The officer quickly lowered his hand. "Of course Director, please excuse me." He said and quickly disappeared.

Launch was now down to nine minutes and Volkov felt the need for a drink of that vodka, to hell with the waiting. He stepped to the table and broke the seal of the first bottle that came to hand. Reaching for a tumbler he poured himself a generous portion of the fiery liquid and took a big drink. Watching him, the others soon followed suit. They could always drink a salute later as well.

As he drank the last of the vodka from the glass in hand and poured another he heard the TV voice again.

"...tri, dva, odin, zashiganiye! ...ignition!"

Aboard the capsule Colonel Borya Zolner glanced to the left at his three men. Soldiers all and experienced cosmonauts, they looked relaxed and unconcerned as the final seconds ticked away. The colonel knew each man well; they all were together on missions before, although this was a new kind of task, an actual military mission.

"So, Dimitri your son was accepted to the polytechnic school you wanted for him?" Borya said, making small talk.

"Da he started in the fall. He seems to like it very much and has made many friends." Dimitri said. Major Petrov was a long time friend of Borya, a good officer and soldier. As a major and a pilot he was second in overall command.

The other two cosmonauts, Captain Arkady Sokolov and Lieutenant Robyert Kozlov were also career soldiers and spacemen.

"Aw jeez, here we go!" Borya said in English as the engine exploded to life. All of them laughed at the familiar phrase used by an American astronaut they all knew from the International Space Station. It was something the American always said when blasting off from the Earth or from the space station back to Earth.

Borya tried to remember the American's name, it was English for Ivan... "Yes it was John, John Cummings, the 'aw jeez' guy." He thought.

John had always preferred the American spaceships to the Russian rocket ships, but sometimes there was no other choice to reach the space station. Remembering the good old days, a smile came to Boyar's lips. He wondered where John was now; if he had a glass of vodka, he would drink a toast to John, the 'aw jeez' guy.

"He's probably retired from the American air force drawing a fat retirement check, and living in Hawaii or Miami Beach." Borya thought with a slight touch of envy.

It was not long before the first stage separated with a bang and the second stage kicked in, the Russian mission to *Barcia* was truly on its way, on its way to a new and exciting world.

NOVEMBER 25, 2049
PLANETARY ARRIVAL PLUS 87 DAYS
ALPHA BASE, BARCIA'S PLANET

Barcia's Planet

"Whether you recognize the U.S. claim or no does not change the facts. You are in Barcian Territorial Space, state your intent." John continued in an intentionally harsh voice.

There was a long pause as the U.S. ship continued to approach the Chinese.

"This is Colonel Li Chao Cheng of the People's Liberation Army. To whom am I speaking?" He asked.

"Colonel John Cummings, United States Air Force and military commander of the U.S. Territory of *Barcia's Planet*." John replied. "I need you to tell me specifically why you are approaching our sovereign soil." He continued.

"I reiterate Colonel Cummings that the PRC does not recognize the U. S. claim to *Barcia's Planet*. We intend to set our spacecraft down on the planet's surface." Colonel Li said.

"I regret the PRC's decision to ignore our right to establish sovereignty over a planetary territory on a planet we discovered, were the first to land upon, and where we have already established a settlement and a government according to maritime law. I cannot allow you to land upon our territory except under certain conditions. You must stand down, for you to proceed otherwise will provoke a military response from us." John replied.

There was a long silence and John's instruments registered the fact that *Dragon* was slowing. Then Colonel Li spoke again.

"And what are those conditions Colonel Cummings?" Li asked.

"You may set down on the planet if your vessel is damaged and in vital need of repairs. Or, if you and your crew are seeking political asylum." John replied. He was pretty sure that the second option was not a viable one for the commander of the *Dragon*.

The silence this time was even longer, and when the answer came, it surprised John.

"The *Dragon* was on its way to Mars as the government of the PRC announced. However, we developed a technical problem with our navigation system and we diverted to *Barcia* where we hoped to seek a friendly port to affect repairs." Li explained.

"So, we would like to take advantage of the first option you offered, repair our ship and either continue on to Mars, or return to Earth." He continued.

John didn't know what he had expected, but it wasn't this. He needed to confer with Doc.

"Please bring your vessel to a halt and standby Colonel Li."

John said, reaching and toggling his radio to the secure link to Alpha Base.

Doc was monitoring the conversation and when Trish nodded John was on the secure frequency he answered.

"What do you think Doc? If we turn them away and they do indeed have a real problem we'll look pretty bad in the eyes of the world." John said.

"I agree with you John, especially if our decision were to lead to the loss of their ship. On the off chance this might happen, I am sending the coordinates where they can land, far enough away from the base they can't surprise attack us, but close enough we can render aid if necessary. Permission to land is granted." Doc said.

"Roger." John quipped, immediately switching to the open channel.

"Very well *Dragon*, the U.S. governor has granted permission for you to enter orbit around the planet and then proceed to the surface at the following coordinates." John said, as he sent the landing site data.

"An appropriate visa is granted for the period of thirty days or until your repairs are completed, whichever is shorter in duration. Initially your crew is quarantined aboard your ship while appropriate access to the planet's surface is decided." John continued.

"Understood *Astraeus* thank you." Colonel Li replied, a smile of satisfaction John of course could not see on his handsome Asian face. Colonel Li, like a good many of his contemporaries, was a direct descendant of the great Genghis Khan. The *Dragon* maneuvered and gained velocity as it swung away on a course to enter an orbit around the planet called *Barcia*.

John kept his spaceship a safe distance away and followed the Chinese into the same orbit. He settled into a routine of follow-the-adversary. John wanted to contact the approaching two American warships but was concerned the Chinese might overhear his transmission, so he waited. Instead he concentrated on the *Dragon*.

NOVEMBER 25, 2049
PLANETARY ARRIVAL PLUS 87 DAYS
BAIKONUR COSMODROME, RUSSIA

"It is a great day for Mother Russia, and for your space agency, eh Director Volkov?" The stout general said in a somewhat slurred voice. The general held a half-full glass of vodka in his right hand, centered in the middle of his chest, beside the spectacular rows of ribbons, sprinkled with a vast number of silver and gold stars.

The last of the three Russian rockets completed safe launches and were now in orbit around the world. They would traverse the well known orbital path enough times to gain the gravitational slingshot to put them on their way to *Barcia's Planet*.

"It is indeed comrade general." Volkov said, falling back into the old vernacular popular when his country was still a part of the Soviet Union.

Volkov and the general saluted one another and drained their glasses. The director was happy to learn that the Chinese 'Mars' ship had reached the contested American planet. The Chinese would serve as a distraction for the Americans as his three ships, soon to be followed by others, also reached the new heavenly body hurtling toward its orbital home in the solar system. Soon, Volkov thought, children everywhere would learn that the sun's family of planets once again was nine.

But, Volkov was very aware of the American fleet of five spaceships even now getting close to the planet. What he didn't know, but was soon to find out, was the nature of two of them. It was these two ships that were to put an end to the Russian attempt to land on *Barcia*. But as one mission was canceled, the ever resilient director would find his ships and their brave crews yet another.

NOVEMBER 25, 2049
PLANETARY ARRIVAL PLUS 87 DAYS
ALPHA BASE, BARCIA'S PLANET

When it happened John was understandably confused, but then his experience as a fighter pilot kicked in and he recognized what Colonel Li had done.

Initially *Astraeus* followed *Dragon* as the Chinese ship cut its engines and 'fell' toward the planet looming large below. As it fell it gained speed until its movement around the globe countered the planet's gravitational pull and it neatly inserted itself into orbit. Soon after, Hal announced the *Dragon's* ground scanning radar was activated.

"They are actively scanning the planet's surface John, as if they are trying to find a particular site." Hal said.

John frowned and then said. "Well, I think that I would do the same thing Hal. No pilot is willing to enter an unknown landing area without at least a cursory radar scan."

"I can understand that but I'm wondering if maybe they are scanning to find a landing site other than the one you gave them." Hal continued.

"That's certainly possible Hal; all we can do is stay close and watch them for any premature maneuver toward *Barcia*." John said as he handed Hal a zero-gee meal. He took one for himself and they settled back to take a break and eat.

Dragon completed one full orbit and began a second when John called them.

"Colonel Li, we want *Dragon* to break orbit as we approach orbital exit point for the coordinates provided you." John said.

"Roger, retrofire minus ten minutes, twenty-eight seconds." Li answered in his almost accent free American English.

John acknowledged and five minutes later he reached and flipped up the cover guard for his own maneuver rockets.

"Retrofire in five minutes, ten seconds." John said, his eyes scanning the ship's instrument panel for any warning lights, a task all pilots did automatically without thought.

"John!" Hal said excitedly. "John they're…they're gone!" Hal yelped.

John's head snapped up and he stared at the view screen. Indeed the *Dragon* was gone! He couldn't help but smile and shake his head in admiration.

"Li's a fighter pilot, the bastard just did a high-gee barrel roll." John said.

"A what? …a high what?" Hal stammered in confusion.

"He knew exactly when my eyes would scan the instrument panel for warning lights. And in that interval he did what a fighter pilot would do to evade an enemy aircraft on his tail."

John paused a moment and looked out his portside viewport. He caught a glimpse of a dark spot against the white clouds of the planet that soon lit up in a fiery flare as it entered the atmosphere.

"A high-gee barrel roll is a defensive maneuver. The pilot angles the nose of his aircraft up into the wind and then applies full rudder and pulls the stick full aft. You bleed off speed and your aircraft goes inverted as it loops back the way you just came. It'll cause the enemy plane behind to pass you like a bullet. You can then maneuver away." John said, unconsciously showing the move with his hands.

"But there's no wind here John. And what does it mean to go inverted?" Hal asked.

"Another way of saying inverted Hal is upside down. Li created his own nose lifting 'wind' by firing his maneuver rockets to push the nose of his spacecraft up. At almost the same time he fired his main engine and went inverted, right over us and then he steered for the planet, all very neat." John said.

Hal seemed to think a moment. "Well, we could do the same thing and follow him couldn't we?" He asked.

"It's too late. The best we can do is circle *Barcia* one more time and exit our orbit at the same place *Dragon* did. Chances are they landed as soon as they possibly could, probably so they could make their own claim for a part of *Barcia* and get it on video." John replied.

"Ah. That way they can counter our claim at the UN with one of their own." Hal said as the meaning of the Chinese action became clear.

John reached and toggled the radio to the fleet's frequency. "*Astraeus* to *Trathen* over." He said, broadcasting in the clear and not using the *Trathen's* call sign.

"*Trathen* here Colonel Cummings. I assume since you're sending in the clear that the cat's out of the bag, over." Tom said.

"It is indeed Commander Phillips. We plan to shoot around the planet again and exit orbit where the *Dragon* did. We will be in position in one hour and twelve minutes, hope you can join the party." John said.

"We can be there with bells on. How did your cat escape?" Tom continued.

"Colonel Li used his maneuver rockets and main engine to affect a high-gee barrel roll right over the top of us." John said, chuckling.

"Well shoot; he must be a veteran fighter pilot!" Tom exclaimed. "See you on the other side. *Trathen* out."

Tom continued as he reached for and pushed the red plunger marked 'GQ' and activated the general quarters klaxon aboard the warship. The calm female voice of the computer came on line at the same time and said:

"General quarters, all hands, general quarters, prepare for action, this is <u>not</u> a drill." At the same time an automatic radio pulse activated the klaxon on the *Black*.

Lucas looked at his co-pilot with a grin as the sexy computer voice said "Attention all hands, the squadron flagship has initiated general quarters, all hands general quarters, prepare for action, this is <u>not</u> a drill!"

"Here we go buddy. Our first off-earth action!" Lucas said in satisfaction.

At Alpha Base Trish picked up her handheld radio and called Doc, who was helping Marjorie with the hydroponics garden.

"Doc here." The territorial governor answered. "What's up Trish?"

"I received an automatic transmission from the Navy squadron's communication system. The two warships have gone to general quarters. Hostilities with the Chinese may be about to commence." Trish said.

Doc paused and glanced at Marjorie who had overheard Trish's transmission.

"Very well, please get Rolf and meet us in the hab." Doc said, already striding toward the building with Marjorie.

The first person they encountered when they entered the hab was Isadora. Because of her close relationship with John both Doc and Marjorie were quite comfortable around her.

The Italian beauty looked up with a smile that embraced them both. "Doc, Marjorie, how pleasant to see you." She said.

"Thanks Isadora, can you get Dr. St. John to join us in the common area, and tell him to please bring all your crew who are not too busy. I'm afraid I have some… distressing news." Doc said.

Isadora nodded; a slight frown of concern crossing her features.

"Yes, of course." She replied.

As Isadora turned to go, first Trish came in shortly followed by an earnest faced Rolf. They trailed Doc as he made his way to the front of the room. The EU crew soon joined them, taking a seat and looking expectantly and with some concern at Doc.

Dr. St. John came in last and nodded solemnly at Doc as he too sat down.

"Thank you all for coming so promptly. Dr. St. John I am speaking to you now in your capacity as the EU's ambassador." Doc began.

"I know that all of you are aware that a resupply fleet composed of five ships is on its way here. What you don't know is that two of those ships are warships." He said, and then paused as a murmur went around the room.

"The two warships are the *U.S.S. Trathen* and the *U.S.S. Black* together they form the *Black Cat Squadron* of the U.S. Navy. They are much larger than a general purpose resupply ship and carry a compliment of five U.S. Army rangers armed with the latest infantry weapons.

I'm sure your government has informed you that the Chinese ship *Dragon*, ostensibly on its way to Mars, diverted from their flight path toward *Barcia*. That vessel, despite being met by the *Astraeus* and directed to an approved landing site on the planet, has evidently triggered a response by our warships.

Exactly what that means I am unsure of at this time. What I can tell you is that I have great confidence in Colonel Cummings and the men of the United States Navy and have no doubt they can protect us from any adversary. Does anyone have any questions?" He asked, and then sighed inside as almost everyone's hand went up.

A little over an hour later, a closely coordinated squadron of three ships lit up the sky of *Barcia.* The air crackled with a mind numbing roar as the three ships descended simultaneously to the surface of the planet.

The Chinese crew of the *Dragon* stood in awe as the planet itself seemed to shake from the tremendous concussive sound. It was so loud all five of the men, two officers and three armed soldiers, toggled their helmet internal sound off.

The scream of rocket engines came through their helmets anyway.

The ships slowly settled on the plain in a three sided triangle around the *Dragon*, their engines continuing to lick fire for a few seconds before flaming out simultaneously.

The ship commanders looked at their view screens and saw the same scene, except but from three separate view points.

The Chinese soldiers each held a rifle at the ready while one of the officers, likely Colonel Li wore a sidearm. The second officer appeared to be a non-military government official. The soldiers and Colonel Li wore white EVA suits trimmed in red with the red and gold squared flag of the PRC on their chests. The official's suit was white trimmed in a neutral blue.

The Chinese looked from ship to ship, noting that two of them were nearly twice the size of the other one.

The three ships sat ominously silent for a number of minutes and the crew of the *Dragon* began to shift about. Then, at a prearranged signal the ramps of the American ships began to swing down with the audible whir of electric motors. Again there was a pause and suddenly six armed men issued from each of the two larger ships as two other men, unarmed, appeared out of the smaller spacecraft.

The eight heavily armed and armored rangers and their four officers wearing side arms and carrying small machineguns took position in two groups facing the Chinese. Stopping for a moment to confer with an officer, the two men from the small ship strode toward the *Dragon*.

John and Hal stopped midway between the Americans and the Chinese and waited. Colonel Li spoke to the official and then they both walked toward them.

As they arrived Colonel Li gave them as snappy a salute as possible in his EVA suit. John returned the military gesture of respect.

"Colonel Cummings I presume." Colonel Li said with a grin and John swore he saw a glint of mischief in his eye.

John quickly wiped his own hint of a smile off his lips and put on his war face, because despite Li's reference to the historical meeting between explorer Henry Morton Stanly and Dr. David Livingstone, this was a serious confrontation.

"Colonel Cummings, may I introduce you to Comrade Sheng Chu Yang of the PRC diplomatic corps." Colonel Li said.

John nodded in return to Yang's abbreviated bow and then addressed the diplomat.

"Mr. Yang, by not obeying my orders as to where to land, your ship has violated Barcian Territorial airspace, you and your crew are illegal aliens on the sovereign soil of the United States. Your visa is hereby terminated. I require you to surrender yourself, your weapons and your ship to the Barcian Territorial Military immediately." John said.

"I can assure you we will do no such thing, the Peoples Republic of China does not recognize the U.S. claim to this planet. If you wish to disarm us it will have to be through the force of arms. I have already claimed the southern half of this continent for the PRC. The official proceedings have already been sent to Earth." Yang replied.

"That is most unfortunate. China has no claim to any of this planet, you did not discover it, and you were not the first nation to land upon it. Since you arrived here illegally, any actions you have taken are illegal. This event is also being filmed and I intend the world to see the arrest of intruders on American soil." John said, his jaw set in a firm line.

Yang did not back down however.

"I reiterate that if you wish to arrest us it will be through the force of arms, if you can prevail." He said.

John raised his right hand over his head and made a fist, a prearranged signal for Commander Phillips. The eyes of the Chinese were now on the Army rangers but they saw no movement. Then something moved on both ramps of the large ships and down came two six-wheeled armored cars that proceeded to either end of the line of rangers and then around them to their front and stopped between the soldiers and the Chinese ship.

Yang looked at the two vehicles with his stony gaze and then returned it to John. Once again John raised his hand and made a fist. Suddenly a section behind the driver's cab came up and snapped into place. Pointing at the intruders were two 37 millimeter high-powered fast firing cannon. Beside each cannon was a heavy .50 caliber machine gun.

"Those cannon and machineguns are automatically fed ammunition stored inside the armored car. Your ship can be turned into a scrap heap in a matter of seconds, and we don't even have to take out a single man of your crew." John said.

Yang fumed but seemed at a loss as to where to go from here.

Colonel Li looked at the not very diplomatic diplomat.

"Comrade Yang, if I may?" He said.

Yang continued to stare with naked hostility at John and then lowered his eyes and nodded.

"Perhaps Colonel Cummings, I could have our soldiers take their firearms and secure them, unloaded, back aboard the *Dragon*. Then, the four of us could retire to our ship for some well deserved tea, and while you are inside our vessel you can observe the wonders of our spaceship and see that our intentions are peaceful."

Colonel Li said, looking once again at Yang who nodded almost imperceptivity.

"This could be done, if your soldiers return outside your ship after securing their weapons and stay where my rangers can see them. I also wish to include my four other officers in your offer of refreshment, I'm sure they would enjoy some excellent tea from China." John said.

"This is acceptable." Li said, not looking at Yang. Then he turned and issued orders to his soldiers. When they returned unarmed from the *Dragon*, Hal walked back to his own officers and brought them forward.

"Gentlemen, the representatives of the Peoples Republic of China have invited us to a social and diplomatic tea." John said.

Yang accepted the terms outlined to him, including a thirty day visa or until the Chinese could repair their navigation system. They were allowed outside their ship as long as they remained in sight of the two Navy ships and carried no weapons.

Video of the peaceful settlement to the confrontation was sent to NASA, as well as the State and Defense Departments. The film was shown publicly and the Russians noted there were now U.S. warships on *Barcia*. The mission of their expedition would have to change.

There were a number of issues to be discussed with Doc, including the status of Colonel Li. After the tea aboard the *Dragon*, Li met with John outside.

"One of the options you mentioned for staying on *Barcia* John, if I may call you John, was political asylum."

"If you are asking for yourself Li, I cannot imagine a scenario where you would not be welcomed by the government of the United States." John replied.

"But, what about your family, will they not suffer reprisals should you defect?" John continued.

"In China I am kind of a…I think the word in English is, a celebrity. I can do almost anything I wish, my wife and children are currently vacationing on Hawaii. Any decision I make will have to include them." Li said.

"Securing your family should be a piece of cake. I will take your proposal to the governor. However, who will pilot *Dragon* back to Earth?" John asked.

"One of Comrade Yang's many talents is that he is a qualified astronaut and ship's pilot. I'm sure he will be successful." Li said.

It was an easy hop for the *Astraeus* from the newly designated Bravo Base on the southern end of the continent back to Alpha Base. The two warships were to remain at the new base at least until the disposition of the Chinese question and maybe longer. When the three supply ships arrived in a day or so it was going to get pretty crowded around Alpha Base.

Hal, ever the planetary scientist, filmed the changed landscape of *Barcia* as they passed over it. The snow was mostly gone from the open plains, replaced by flowing creeks and small rivers. Some glacier melt in the mountains could be seen and the melt water was forming lakes and adding to the free flow of water. A faint tint of green was visible as the native plants were spreading, their seeds and spores borne along in the wind and water. There was no doubt that *Barcia* was growing into a true, and almost nearly identical, twin of Earth.

Carefully setting down the *Astraeus*, John and Hal went through the post-flight shutdown procedures, donned their EVA suits and headed for the airlock. The outer doors opened and the ramp began its descent to the ground. As it came down they could see the rest of the crew as well as Isadora waiting for them. Hal and John did a double take, because their friends were standing and smiling at them, and not one of them was wearing a helmet or EVA suit! Instead, they were dressed in NASA blue coveralls with jackets and dark blue watch caps. All that is except Isadora who was dressed in the same manner but wearing the EU's red coveralls.

They all began to applaud and yelling "Yea, yea, the air pressure has reached normal for earthlings!"

The two returning astronauts quickly strode down the ramp, turning off their internal air system and removing their helmets.

"Aw jeez, what a great welcome home, and on Thanksgiving Day too!" John said feeling the wind on his face for the first time in many, many months.

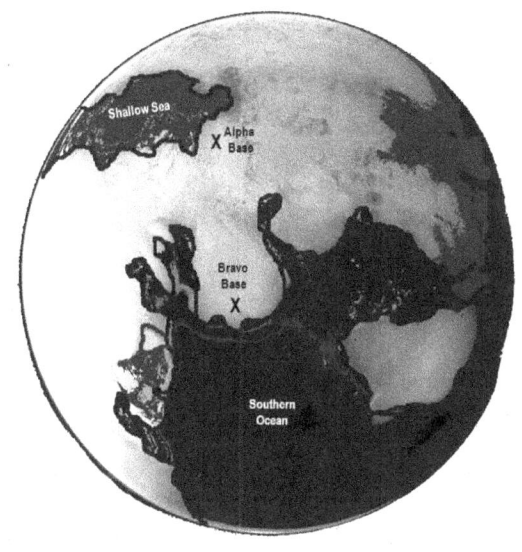

NOVEMBER 28, 2049
PLANETARY ARRIVAL PLUS 90 DAYS
HEADQUARTERS ROSCOSMOS, MOSCOW

Boris Volkov set the old fashioned telephone back in its cradle. Old fashioned it appeared, but it was secured and encrypted with the latest available software and was connected directly to the Kremlin.

The premier himself told him about the American warships on *Barcia*. He and Boris knew his men in their space capsule would have no chance of getting past the Americans to land on the prodigal moon. That was the latest theory on the origin of *Barcia*, and one that seemed both plausible and fit the known facts.

Boris agreed with the premier's conclusion but pointed out that his men could land upon and occupy *Barcia's* moon, Phobos. A station there Boris said, figuratively between Earth and *Barcia*, could be a very useful chip to play in the developing game of space chess.

Premier Nikolas Fedorov was a lover of the game of chess, and the real power broker in Russia. Without conferring with the mostly impotent Russian president, he approved the suggested change of mission. If it turned out to be a bad decision, he could always blame Boris for misleading him.

Boris summoned Elena and told her to schedule an immediate meeting of the department leaders or their first deputies.

"And tell them I don't want to see any first deputies!" He added, which was unnecessary, because Elena already knew that. Elena was not beautiful, that would be a distraction to Boris, but she was smart, and she knew her director.

Fifteen minutes later Boris was sitting at the head of the large conference room table. He was pretending to be immersed in the paperwork before him, but actually he was noting the arrival of each of his department heads. Finally he sat back and looked up. Everyone was in his designated seat except Gurkin. Boris frowned, and then scowled as the now late, mousey looking engineer made his way to his chair in the middle on the table's left side.

Boris glared at him a moment and then cleared his throat. His head swiveled as he noted each man and then he nodded as he saw no first deputies among them.

"We have a change of mission." Boris said, his words eliciting several surprised looks.

"Our Chinese friends have informed us the clever Americans have two warships on *Barcia*."

He paused as there came a low mummer from the group of scientists, engineers, and military men.

"Each warship has a compliment of U.S. Army rangers commanded by naval officers. If you are unfamiliar with the rangers, they are the toughest soldiers of America's armed forces. These men are heavily armed and have armored vehicles at their disposal. At this time they have not occupied Phobos, the new planet's new moon. We are going to occupy Phobos." Boris said and then waited patiently for the excited but hushed conversations to die down.

"We need all the hard data we can get on Phobos, especially all photographs and radar scans of its surface. Upon arrival, we will lay claim to this moon. From this Russian rock in space we will become a, to use an American phrase, a pain in the ass!" Boris said and was rewarded by a round of laughter and light applause.

The mousey engineer, Gurkin, signaled he wished to speak and Boris reluctantly nodded at him.

"Director Volkov, the Americans visited Phobos in the past." He said and then glanced down at his notes.

"Yes, in 2047 their 'Moon-Grazer' mission landed and explored Phobos. Will this not complicate any claim we may make?" He asked.

"Of course it will." Boris replied.

"But there is another American saying that says possession is nine-tenths of the law. We, comrade Gurkin, will posses Phobos. Let's get to work."

DECEMBER 3, 2049
RUSSIAN MISSION TO BARCIA'S MOON
IN ORBIT AROUND PHOBOS

Phobos

Borya studied the visual display of Phobos, the computer added latitude and longitude lines for easy navigation reference. The Stickney Crater was centered in the picture. The huge crater was the dominant feature on this moon's surface.

The computer generated a simulated inter-pretation of the small moon, giving the display a cartoon-like appearance. There was no mistaking the debris orbiting just above the moon surface, the result of Barcia ripping Phobos from Mars. That violent act stirred up the ancient dust and rocks, and with Phobos' weak gravitational pull it had not yet completely settled.

Borya recalled the literature he'd read on Phobos. Phobos was discovered in 1877 by an American astronomer with the odd biblical name of Asaph Hall. Naming the moon Phobos, Hall then spotted the large crater he named *Stickney* after his wife Angelina's maiden name. It also bore the designation Mars 1, but that name was now obsolete.

While the satellite of Mars, Phobos orbited very close, only 3,700 miles from the Red Planet's surface. When it settled around *Barcia* it took a longer path and now circled its new home world in a still wobbly orbit at about 5,400 miles away. Most planetary scientists, including Dr. Halberd Boyle currently on *Barcia*, agreed that orbit would decay over time to about half that distance.

Capsule 3126 approached the moon of *Barcia* directly with capsules 3125 and 3127 following behind like ducklings as there was no need to orbit Phobos before landing. The moon appeared exactly as the American reports of 2047 described it. The tiny moon had a radius of only 11 kilometers and was irregular in shape. If it were roaming free through space it would be simply another medium-to-small sized asteroid. The fact that Phobos orbited a planet gave it the lofty designation of a moon.

The Russian landing site was facing both the light of the sun and the three oncoming spaceships. The landing appeared straightforward although Borya expected them to encounter a debris-laden though almost non-existent 'atmosphere', near the moon's surface.

"Two thousand kilometers and closing." Lieutenant Robyert Kozlov announced.

Captain Arkady Sokolov followed him with "Deceleration burn in two minutes and 32 seconds."

"Separation from orbiter coming up on 11 minutes at my mark. Mark!" Major Petrov added.

Borya then added "Very well." and he then spoke into the radio.

"Five and seven deploy and match your telemetry with the command lander."

Looking out the view ports on either side of the lander Borya watched them come on line. The three landers would separate simultaneously from the three orbiters, leaving one cosmonaut in each orbiter. Robyert was their designated cosmonaut to stay aboard and maintain their orbiter; he smoothly rose from his seat, paused to give them a salute, and disappeared to the rear of the vessel.

Once detached the orbiters, belying their name, would not orbit Phobos but move away to take up a stationary position some distance away.

The landers separated from one another with their maneuvering rockets until they were in a triangular formation about fifty meters from one another. And that is how they would land on the plain, about three kilometers to the left of Stickney Crater.

The weak gravitational pull of Phobos dictated they had to land softly to keep from bouncing off the moon's surface. Thanks to the American data from 2047 they knew exactly what speed they needed to use in their approach to touchdown.

Their descent was so slow that if there was someone on Phobos watching them come in for a landing, they would quickly get bored with waiting.

After separating it took the three landers an hour and a half to 'fall' to the moon surface. And that is how it went, slow but perfect in completion. A twenty second 'puff' from their maneuvering rockets was all that was needed to slow for a gentle touchdown. Five reported grazing a boulder with one of the lander's legs that set them to slowly spinning but they got down with little real trouble.

The landing was kind of anticlimactic and the celebration was somewhat muted and more a relief than anything else.

"I bet this doesn't look anything like it did two years ago when the yanks landed here." Arkady said looking out the left viewport into the dust filled air.

"Yeah well, the Americans could land in a pile of yak dung in Siberia and find an Eden underneath." Dimitri quipped.

"Okay, you two get on with the shutdown procedures, I'm gonna go EVA and check Five's lander leg. We don't want any surprises." Borya said.

"After you shut down you guys get some rest, take four hours. We'll set up the habitation configuration after that." Borya said, and then he was out the airlock.

"I love that guy." Arkady said. "He's always, always, looking out for his men."

"Best damn colonel in the Russian military." Dimitri quipped nodding his head.

When Borya reached lander Five he quickly ascertained that any damage to the leg was minor. He looked up at the viewport and saw one of the men looking out at him with a smile. Giving him thumbs up Borya indicated he wanted to come in. The watching cosmonaut's smile went even broader.

The crew of this lander had already started to convert their ship to the habitation configuration.

The interior consisted of folding modular areas that slid out of the way when not needed. Sliding accordion dividers were then opened to make separate 'rooms'. There was a small galley complete with a table where all three men could sit at the same time. Because one cosmonaut was expected to be awake at all times there was only two sleeping cells that closed off with their own sliding doors. There was also a relaxation pod that unfolded outside the ship for video viewing or tablet reading and also doubled as an isometric exercise area. With such light gravity they needed to exercise regularly to keep muscle tone and bone density at required levels.

The gravity of Phobos was so light the cosmonauts found they had to move very carefully or find themselves smashing into the ceiling or bulkheads.

"I see you three have decided to get settled in before you rest. That's fine; we'll run through two four-hour rest periods and then hold a ceremony on the moon's surface." Borya said.

After receiving their report on the status of their lander Borya returned to his own lander and discovered Arkady and Dimitri also did not rest before converting the ship to habitation mode. Borya took the first watch and the two other men retired to what privacy the sleep rooms provided.

Toggling the computer Borya read the status report for the lander he had not visited. Satisfied, he then brought up the claim of sovereignty document and memorized its wording. He spent the rest of the watch scanning the nearby surface of Phobos.

Like Earth's moon this moon was also mostly white rocks and dust broken up by the occasional darker chunk of material. There were craters of different sizes in almost every direction. Luckily the spot they landed upon had only small craters nearby. The dust seemed to just hang in the air, but Borya knew it was slowly settling.

Looking back toward Earth's location he could see thousands of stars in the distance and the one tinged blue was his home world. It would continue to grow in size as the planetary system consisting of *Barcia* and Phobos moved closer to conjunction with Earth and the sun. When *Barcia* rose as the moon slowly rotated, it was truly magnificent. Although he had seen the Earth-like planet as they came into the system and was impressed, it was even more impressive now.

Phobos' orbit was not a perfect circle and he was seeing *Barcia* from the moon's closest approach to the planet. He could see continents, islands, seas, oceans and even rivers. The blue skies, like those of Earth boasted white clouds of water vapor that sailed around the planet. He marveled at its close resemblance to his own world and was determined that Russia would get its own foothold on this, from all reports, fully functional and human friendly planet. The second home of all mankind.

Although not religious himself, Borya recalled a passage he' read spoken by Jesus. "In my father's house there are many mansions. I go there now to prepare a place for you." Evidently *Barcia* was one of those mansions.

When Arkady rose to relieve him Borya entered the sleeping quarters and lay down, but he slept only fitfully.

Four hours later the men in all three landers were up and ready. It was not normal procedure for all cosmonauts to be out of their ships at once. But the Kremlin wanted a show of strength on the surface of Phobos during the ceremony. The camera on each lander was filming from the three different viewpoints. The white, blue, and red of the Russian tricolor was stretched on the usual pole and arm set up for use on airless moons or asteroids. Borya stood beside the flag and after receiving and returning the salute of the assembled cosmonauts, solemnly read the proclamation that not only lay claim to Phobos, but denounced the American claim to all of *Barcia*.

Returning to the lander Borya made sure that the film from all the landers were sent to Moscow.

That evening the film aired on international and interplanetary TV, just before the Russian ambassador read the Phobos proclamation to the UN General Assembly. The membership rose to applaud, all except the ambassadors from the US and the EU.

When the US ambassador rose and stood at the podium to protest the Russian action inside the territorial space declared by the U.S. his short-lived speech was booed to silence.

Phobos belonged to Russia, but the jewel that was *Barcia* was firmly in the grasp of America and her ally the European Union. The lines of demarcation and discord were drawn.

And in the inky depths of space, closer than anyone realized, the wandering planet, Earth's prodigal moon, drew near its fated rendezvous with Sol and mankind.

DECEMBER 23, 2049
PLANETARY ARRIVAL PLUS 115 DAYS
THE CAPITOL OF BARCIA, ALPHA CITY

John strode around the newly renamed Alpha City, designated the territorial capitol of *Barcia*. The place was bustling with new people and many more of the small earth movers and newly arrived transports. Doc was recently promoted from acting governor to governor of the Territory of *Barcia's Planet*.

Three resupply ships stood beside *Beagle* and *Astraeus* in the area that was now called Alpha City Spaceport. Two more ships were expected to arrive both at the city and at Bravo Base, newly designated a permanent military base, with Commander Tom Phillips in charge. Two more habitations were nearly complete at both sites with others going up soon.

In the middle of the city, like an agricultural city park, was Marjorie's Garden. It was exploding with produce that included corn, beans and carrots and even tomatoes. The soil was incredibly productive with the free flowing water and the warmth of the sun all that was needed. Temperatures had modulated to those of late spring on Earth and the 'alien' plants from the home world thrived.

Scientists were calling for more research into the native animals discovered near the smoke columns. But there was just too much to do for everyone currently on the planet. The EU with the agreement of the US was sending more supply ships along with engineers and more embassy personnel.

The latest projections using orbital mechanics indicated *Barcia's* final inner solar system orbit would be slightly inside that of Earth. This meant it would be several thousands of miles closer to the sun relieving any fears that it might collide with Earth. *Barcia* would take up a position a little more than half way around the sun from Earth. This would make it either behind or in front of the home world depending upon your point of view. Kind of like a glass half full or half empty kind of thing.

The Chinese ship left *Barcia* two days ago with Colonel Li, now Mr. Li, aboard Tom Phillip's ship the *Trathen.* Li was scheduled to come to Alpha City soon where his wife and family would join him, traveling as passengers aboard one of the supply ships. Li was a Department of Defense civilian employee now, serving as a special consultant. Inadvertently Li and his family were going to be the first settler-immigrants to *Barcia*. Li felt that the new planet would be the safest place for his family, far away and well protected from any threat on Earth.

More government employees were on their way including surveyors, engineers, doctors, administrators and many others.

Conventional construction of housing, offices and other structures fell under the Army Corps of Engineers and in the case of Bravo Base, the Navy's Seabee battalions.

Cartographers were already busy mapping and searching the best planetary sites for settlements. The government wanted to start immigration from the U.S. and the EU to start in one year's time.

Environmental scientists, biologists and botanists were concerned about native plants and animals and the impact human occupation might have on them. They were researching the planet's ecology as quickly as possible, it was a tall order.

Cameras, sensors and telescopes were set up both on *Barcia* and Earth to observe and document the passing of the prodigal moon on its journey to the inner solar system.

John and Isadora, newly engaged, planned on a wedding with photographs and films that showed passing Earth as the background to their vows.

They would be joined by another couple, Trish and Rolf also became engaged; somewhat belatedly as Trish announced she was pregnant. Their child would be the first person born on *Barcia's Planet*. And although they knew the sex of the first native born citizen of the territory, they weren't telling anyone.

And as the time drew nearer for the union of Earth and its prodigal moon, everyone watched the night sky.

FEBRUARY 28, 2050
PLANETARY ARRIVAL PLUS 180 DAYS
ALPHA CITY, BARCIA'S CAPITOL

At first the Earth seen from *Barcia* appeared as a blue speck and the moon could not be seen with the naked eye. But every night cameras tracked the blue speck that became a blue bead and then a blue marble with a pearl white companion, both nestled in a sea of brightly shining stars.

Trish Barcia found herself the most popular person on the wandering planet. There were at least a thousand people on the planet now and it seemed to her that every one of them stopped by to meet her, the discoverer of humankind's second home, and to shake her hand. She felt like a politician.

Although she was flattered of course, it was a little overwhelming and disrupted her important work. As the lead astronomer she was organizing, with Rolf's help, the viewing, scanning, and recording of the event dubbed "The Conjunction".

At its nearest approach *Barcia* would come within five hundred thousand miles of Earth, close enough to view well but not close enough to cause any disruption. They were two blue marbles passing in the light of their mutual sun.

Sixty-five million years in the making, the conjunction of Earth and *Barcia* did not disappoint.

The two planets, both the children of Sol, swam first toward and then past one another. One would continue on its billions of years old trek around the sun and through the stars. The other would take up a closer and new, yet familiar, path around the life giving sun.

Eyes alight with intelligence, a species not yet around when she had left, watched the prodigal moon return to, if only a moment, its parent planet.

Views of Earth and the moon from *Barcia* were exchanged for views of *Barcia* and its moon. The pictures were eerily similar and people watched them side by side in amazement, and looked at one another with huge grins on their faces.

They weren't sure why they felt so elated, nor could they explain the overwhelming feeling of relief. But psychologists would later say it was a visceral feeling as the viewers realized that human beings now trod upon and lived upon two separate life supporting worlds. Never again would a single cosmic event ever threaten the existence of humans with mass extinction.

Left unvoiced was the knowledge too that one day, one day very soon, there would be two equal and independent worlds within a human controlled planetary system. Barcia was an insurance policy and another step for mankind toward the eternal stars.

APRIL 20, 2050
PLANETARY ORBIT, PLUS 0 DAYS
ALPHA CITY, BARCIA'S PLANET

The original crew of *Astraeus* stood around a visibly pregnant Trish Barcia-Earhart as she sat in the ship's command center.

"Go ahead Trish; NASA's waiting to hear from you." Doc said with a big smile.

"*Astraeus* to ground control, over." Trish said, rotating her chair to face her friends. Besides Doc there was Hal, Marjorie, Rolf of course, John and Isadora.

"Ground control *Astraeus* go ahead." A voice on the radio replied.

"Ground control, please be advised that *Astraeus* and the planet currently stuck to its tail fins, has achieved orbit around the sun." Trish said with a big smile.

"We copy *Astraeus*, thank you for a job well done and congratulations from the team here at NASA and ground control. From this moment on your communications will be directly with NASA Headquarters at the Johnson Space Center in Houston. Goodbye *Astraeus*."

247

In the command center, everyone cheered and patted Trish gently on her shoulder. After all, she was with child.

The End

Since you finished reading this book you must have either enjoyed it or found it interesting or perhaps with any luck, both. So, you should watch for the sequel to *Prodigal Moon* currently being written with the working title of:

BARCIA'S PLANET

This book is about the exploration and settlement of mankind's second planetary home. To view this book and others, read a preview and see the cover you can go here: www.lulu.com/greenpheon7

ABOUT THE AUTHOR

A published author for more than a decade, Walt Cross has written many non-fiction books. *Prodigal Moon* is his first science fiction novel.

Walt holds degrees in both history and science and his bestselling book to date is *Custer's Lost Officer; the Search for Lieutenant Henry Moore Harrington, 7th U.S. Cavalry.* It is the biography of a young lieutenant who served with great valor under George Armstrong Custer for four years before his death at the Battle of the Little Big Horn. A reviewer of this book on Amazon wrote:

...Great detective work on the part of author Walt Cross...if you want an "inside" look at an enigmatic CSI style investigative work, it's a great book for you.

R. McNealy

Other reviewers wrote:

Through your persistent and skillful detective work...you solved a major [130 year old] *Little Bighorn mystery.*

> Dr. Gregory J. Urwin, Temple University.

Congratulations...it's a major accomplishment!

> Dr. P. Willey
> California State University

Astounding scholarship!

> Dr. Stephen Bennett
> University of Southern Indiana

Until this book was written Henry Harrington was only a footnote to history. Now he has taken his rightful place among American heroes. *Custer's Lost Officer...* is available online or direct (and signed), from the author.

www.ingramcontent.com/pod-product-compliance
Lightning Source LLC
Chambersburg PA
CBHW072220170626
46813CB00003B/1026